PYRAMID
VOYAGERS

ROY POND
PYRAMID VOYAGERS

Rescue mission to the tombs and
treasures of Egypt's past

AN ALBATROSS BOOK

© Roy Pond 1991

Published in Australia and New Zealand by
Albatross Books Pty Ltd
PO Box 320, Sutherland
NSW 2232, Australia
in the United States of America by
Albatross Books
PO Box 131, Claremont
CA 91711, USA
and in the United Kingdom by
Lion Publishing
Peter's Way, Sandy Lane West
Littlemore, Oxford OX4 5HG, England

First edition 1991

National Library of Australia
Cataloguing-in-Publication data

Pyramid Voyagers

ISBN 0 86760 131 0 (Albatross)
ISBN 0 7459 2185 X (Lion)

I. Title

A823.3

Cover illustration: Michael Mucci
Printed and bound by The Book Printer, Victoria

Contents

1

Digging up the past

SOMETHING WAS MOVING across the covers of Phillip's bed.

He explored the sensation distantly, without opening his eyes. It wasn't the dog. It was too small to be the dog. It wasn't a cat; they didn't own a cat.

With the gateway to his dreams still partly open, bizarre possibilities leaked into Phillip's mind. These possibilities all concerned his long-term interest in Egypt's past. He pictured the hand of an Egyptian mummy, trailing bandages, creeping over the covers.

No, the thing on his bed did not creep. He pictured a king cobra rearing over him, its hood outspread like a reptilian pharaoh. No, it didn't slither.

It paced. It was going around the edges of his bed in a measured way, each step making a stab in the covers like a needle putting in stitches. The thought pinned Phillip's arms to his sides, sealing him under the covers.

Dreading what he might see, he lifted his head a fraction off the pillow, opening his eyes no wider than slits so as not to let in too much of a shock. He saw a bird on his bed. It paced on long legs like a stork, but it was no earthly bird. It emitted the green luminescence of a computer screen. The glow gave a green tinge to its black head and neck and to the brilliant white feathers of its body.

It was an ibis bird, of the kind that appeared in ancient Egyptian hieroglyphs. The sacred ibis.

It laughed at him like a squawking parrot. That made Phillip open his eyes properly. It turned its head to one side in order to train a single eye on him as hard as the bead on a rifle sight, throwing its long, black curve of a beak into profile. The beak did not move, yet Phillip heard the bird speak.

'So you think you are finished with the past, do you, boy? Well, I've brought bad news. The past has come back with a vengeance.'

'Go away. I don't care about the past.'

'You can't turn away from the past any more than you can live in it.'

Phillip shifted uncomfortably as he thought about his recent sojourn in the ancient Egyptian underworld, prompted by his late Uncle William's gift to him of a mummified ibis bird.

'I've left the past behind. What are you doing here? Why have you come back to bother me again?'

'You must recover my body from the earth where it is buried. Your dog buried my mummified remains in the park after your journey to the underworld and now the soil is rotting my costly bandages and dissolving the rare unguents that preserve me.'

'I'm not digging you up,' Phillip said firmly.

'I will reward you by helping you.'

'You can't help me. You're a pagan thing with no

power. I know where real power comes from and it's not from birds and animals or weird-looking idols with heads of birds or crocodiles or jackals.'

'You are going to need my help.'

'I don't need your help.'

'Yes, you do. You are in great danger.'

'What sort of danger?'

'From the past,' the ibis bird said.

'How can the past be a danger?'

'By disappearing. By never having existed.'

'Who would care?'

'You would care. So would everyone in the world. Imagine the world today if ancient Egypt had never existed. Imagine how poor the world would be without ancient Egypt's legacy.'

'I wouldn't care. No more pyramids, tombs and mummies in dusty old museums. So what? I'm sick of it all.'

'Egypt is much, much more. Think, boy. The very word "paper" comes from papyrus, an ancient Egyptian invention. Ancient Egypt gave us paper and spread writing throughout the world. Think of a world without writing!'

Phillip thought about it. 'Great. There'd be no homework.'

'You are not being very sensible. Think a bit further. Without Egypt there would have been no Moses and without Moses there would have been no Exodus and with no Exodus, no Israel and if there were no Israel. . . well. . .' The bird trailed off. 'I'm a pagan bird so I'm not going to spell out what a world without Israel would mean.'

'It doesn't matter now. It's ancient history. I never

want to see a trace of ancient Egypt again. I'm finished with the past. I've learnt my lesson.'

'Have you? You may have stopped living in the past, but now you are doing something far worse – you are denying the past.'

'Yes, I am denying it — and you. Ancient Egypt can disappear for all I care.'

The bird appeared to wince. 'I fear you may get your wish, boy, but know this: it would be a terrible curse if the past were to disappear.'

'No it wouldn't. It would be a relief. The past should be dead and buried, the way you're supposed to be. I don't mean to be unkind, but you are dead, so please go away.'

'You'll need to call on me — and on the past — very soon, you'll see.'

'Goodbye.'

The ibis bird hunched its wings in a shrug. 'Have it your way for now, but remember my warning.'

The glow surrounding the sacred ibis bird went out like a computer screen, sucked away to a bright spot of light before vanishing. He felt the bird spring off the bed and heard the flapping of wings as it rose in the darkness above him.

He woke up with Dogstar, his pharaoh hound, whining fretfully and licking his cheek.

Sunlight shafted into the bedroom. It was morning and another school day. The dream flew away from his waking mind as quickly as the bird had departed. Phillip sat up and swung his legs over the edge of the bed. The dog whined and pawed the rug in a digging motion.

'What's the matter, 'Star boy?' He patted the dog affectionately. Dogstar was looking thin. In fact, the animal was fading away, he thought.

A tall running hound of ancient Egyptian origin and a relative of the greyhound, the pharaoh hound was supposed to be lean as a lightning streak, but now the light-and-tan-coloured dog was showing more bones than an X-ray plate. Perhaps it was time Dogstar paid a visit to the vet.

Dogstar sank to the carpet and sat with its front paws outstretched like a sphinx. With its long ears pricked up like spear tips, it looked like Anubis, the ancient Egyptian jackal of the dead. Phillip could not get away from ancient Egypt. Egypt was always with him in the shape of Dogstar.

As Phillip looked at the dog, the edges of the animal softened and blurred like a view refracted through tears. Were his eyes still bleary from sleep or was the dog really fading away? He blinked again. The image of the dog cleared.

Something came back to him then, not the dream of the bird but images of another time in a dimly remembered place. A store of memories began to whirr and turn like a slide carousel, throwing images with lamplit clarity onto a screen in his mind.

He saw himself in that underworld place of passageways and gateways peopled by monster guardians, giant apes, taskmasters and pagan gods. He saw bare-chested men in white kilts who had jackals' and birds' heads on their broad shoulders. He saw winged creatures called soul birds that had the bodies of birds and the heads of men with wispy beards attached to their chins and he also saw twin goddesses with painted eyes who swung swords with blades shaped like feathers.

He saw himself running with Dogstar, Julia, Barry Coomber and Willard Chase, the archaeological detective — fleeing from danger.

He shivered. He had faced harrowing tests in that underworld place and he had learnt how dangerous it was to live in the past.

Shut the memories away. That was something he had been trying to do ever since his tomb travelling adventures, hoping to forget the past. It was time to get ready for school.

A blizzard of paper aeroplanes filled the air. Their history teacher was late. It was the first lesson of the day and class discipline quickly slipped from disorder into chaos. Phillip twisted his head to look up.

The air space above his head carried a volume of air traffic that would have perturbed an airport control tower operator. He quickly ducked as a paper dart thrown by Barry Coomber, the 'school heavy', tried to dock itself in his ear. It bounced off the side of Phillip's head and landed on his desk.

Julia, who sat in a desk next to Phillip's, directed a deeply pitying stare on Coomber and gave a sorrowful shake of her head, the movement swinging two plaits of dark hair that dangled on the sides of her face. Her look told Barry Coomber that she was truly saddened by his display of arrested mental development.

He scowled back at her. She knew how to annoy the red-faced boy with the shiny eyes. So did Phillip, who picked up Coomber's paper missile and examined it from various angles as if to admire its superior craftsmanship, before thoughtfully crushing it into a ball. Coomber gave him a look that marked him for further trouble.

They heard the growl of an engine outside the classroom as a car arrived in the teachers' parking lot, its tyres squealing as it braked.

'Patchy's coming!' someone said.

Mr Patrick, their history teacher, had arrived. There was a scramble to clean up the paper wreckage of numerous crash sites around the classroom.

A car door opened and then banged shut, closed rather more firmly than usual by Mr Patrick. Their new history teacher drove a red Alfa Romeo, his most prized possession, and he usually nursed it like a baby. Fittingly for a history teacher, it was an old model and the bodywork showed patches of rust. Still, it was a foreign car with a sporty air and that was rare enough at their school.

Mr Patrick swept into the classroom like a gust of wind, slamming the door behind him.

'Good morning, Mr Patrick,' the class said.

'Morning,' he said abruptly, not willing to concede the 'good' part. His face looked like a bowl of cold porridge. Mr Patrick peeled off his coat, a favourite sports jacket with leather patches at the elbows that always made Phillip think of the rust patches on his car. Instead of hanging up the jacket carefully as he usually did, he tossed it onto the rack in the corner of the classroom. Plainly, something had upset their history teacher.

'Sorry to hold up your education, history lovers,' he said in a tight voice, 'but I received a bit of a shock this morning. I woke up to find my car had been vandalised in the night. Some genius has souvenired my Alfa Romeo badge off the front. Taken a screwdriver to the grille to lever it off.'

Barry Coomber put up his hand. 'How much is an Alfa badge worth, Mr Patrick?'

'I don't know, but in nuisance value, a great deal.'

'How much would it be worth to you?' the boy said.

'Why?'

Barry Coomber shrugged. 'Just interested. I wondered how much you'd pay for a new one. You never know. One of us may come across a spare Alfa Romeo badge.'

The teacher's face sharpened suspiciously. 'How would a high school student come across a spare Alfa Romeo badge?'

Phillip could imagine Mr Patrick's thoughts. Was it possible? Would one of his own pupils have the cheek to steal the badge off his car and then try to sell it back to him? The cold porridge face quivered.

'Don't let me discover that one of my pupils took the badge off my car! Never provoke a history teacher, Coomber. They know how to make people suffer. History is filled with violent events and with acts of unspeakable cruelty and history teachers remember them all!'

It was a marvellous threat. Phillip imagined Mr Patrick stretching Coomber's bulky figure on the rack, leaving him for a spell in the Black Hole of Calcutta before burning him at the stake as a martyr and finally cutting off his head at the guillotine. The thought cheered Phillip.

'Don't look at me, Mr Patrick,' Barry Coomber said defensively. Mr Patrick was doing exactly that.

Phillip and Julia exchanged knowing glances. If Coomber wasn't the culprit, then his brother Terry Coomber probably was. Coomber's older brother had already spent a term in a youth detention centre as a result of stealing car parts. Whisperers in the schoolyard said that after his release, Terry had gone straight — straight back to stealing car parts. They also said that he had a name for his illegal business. Midnight Spares. Bad habits ran in Barry Coomber's family.

Mr Patrick seemed to see the hopelessness of making accusations. He shrugged his shoulders slackly. 'Tell you what, Coomber, you find me an Alfa badge and it's worth ten dollars to you, but don't go out and take it off somebody else's car.'

'I wouldn't do that, Mr Patrick,' Coomber said in a wheedling voice, the other voice he used when he wasn't bullying. 'You know me better than that.'

'Perhaps. But don't go telling people I asked you to get me a new badge.'

'I won't.'

'Enough of my problems,' Mr Patrick said, sweeping the class with a look that challenged them. 'Let's give you history lovers a few. Out with your textbooks. Turn to ancient Egypt — burial customs and practices.'

Coomber sat just ahead of Phillip and when the boy lifted his desk lid, Phillip gaped as he saw a row of car badges stuck to the underside with putty glue. A Mercedes Benz three-pointed star in a circle. A Jaguar symbol. A Volvo badge. Barry Coomber felt Phillip's stare. He rounded and gave him a wink, followed by a warning glare. Then, screened from the sight of the teacher by the desk lid, he proceeded to pull an Alfa

Romeo badge out of his right ear like a magic trick.

Coomber was always clever with his hands, but a bit stupid with his spare time, Phillip thought. He was going the same way as his brother Terry — and his father who had also served a gaol term, according to the whisperers.

Couldn't people break away from their past? Did their backgrounds have to imprison them? Phillip wondered about the array of car badges he had seen under the lid of Coomber's desk. Had Coomber stolen them himself? Or had his brother given them to him? Coomber took out his history book and closed the desk lid, cutting short Phillip's speculations.

Phillip looked for his own history book. He found it buried under other books. Once it would have been on top. He opened the book reluctantly and searched for the section on ancient Egyptian burial customs and practices. Once, the book would have automatically fallen open at ancient Egypt through constant use, but that was before the journey. Now the past was something he avoided.

Ancient history. Those two words said it all. Who cared about it? You had to live in the here and now. Wasn't that what he had learnt?

Mr Patrick posed a question to the class. 'Who can explain to me the economic side-benefit of Egypt's funerary practice of burying treasure along with dead pharaohs?'

Phillip knew the answer, but he couldn't be bothered to give it. He sat back in his chair, leaving it to others. Julia prodded him with a glance. This was his subject. Julia knew it. The whole class knew it. Even Mr Patrick knew it. When there was no answer from the class, Mr Patrick singled him out. 'Phillip Simpson, kindly help us out.'

Phillip shrugged. In a voice that started out sounding flat and bored, but gained some animation as he warmed to his subject, he said: 'Egypt produced vast amounts of gold and gemstones from her desert mines as well as exacting tonnes of treasure in tribute from her vassal states. The oversupply could have produced disastrous inflation if the Egyptians hadn't buried so much of it along with their dead, keeping gold and gemstones and other precious commodities out of circulation. Thus Egypt's peculiar funerary practice had a stabilising effect on the economy.'

To the rest of the class it sounded as if Phillip were reading aloud from his textbook. 'In later times, when the tombs were robbed, the oversupply of precious goods on the market helped to hasten Egypt's decline.'

'Thankyou, Simpson. But I should try not to sound so bored with my knowledge if I were you.'

'I'm sorry, but I don't see the point of knowing all this ancient history stuff. It won't help me get a job when I leave school. How can what happened thousands of years ago make any difference to us today?'

He found an unexpected ally in Barry Coomber. 'Too right. First smart thing Phillip Simpson's ever said.'

Mr Patrick looked shaken by Phillip's challenge. It came from a most surprising quarter. Phillip Simpson was the last boy in the world he would have expected to pooh-pooh history. It startled Mr Patrick as much as the loss of his precious Alfa Romeo badge.

'I'm sorry you think that, Simpson, deeply sorry, but

I must tell you that you are gravely mistaken. The past is our great teacher. Consider the Bible. Events in the Bible happened thousands of years ago, too. Don't you think they matter? It has been well said that nations with no sense of history will be condemned to relive it.'

'I used to think the past was important, but not any more.'

'Does this mean you'll be boycotting our excursion to the national museum tomorrow, Simpson? If you don't want to go with us, please tell me now. I'm sure I can provide some written work for you to do in class.'

'I'll go,' Phillip said in a resigned voice.

'I'm gratified,' Mr Patrick said.

Julia's eyes were questioning Phillip again. After school, on the way home, she challenged him. 'I know I used to say you were weird because you were always reading about ancient Egypt and mummies and horrible things like that, but you didn't have to change so much. You're allowed to like ancient Egypt a bit. You don't have to turn against it completely. Now you're being weird in a different way.'

'It doesn't count in my life any more. The past is best forgotten.'

The street outside their school was choked with traffic — parents stopping in cars to pick up their children and rattling school buses lining up outside for students to clamber on board. Julia stepped out of the way of a girl who cut across the pavement to meet her mother in a parked car at the curb. The girl jumped into the car and kissed her mother affectionately.

Julia stared at the girl and her mother and a frown clouded her face. She surprised Phillip by suddenly agreeing with him. 'Perhaps you're right. Perhaps the past is best forgotten.'

A dead note in her voice stirred Phillip's interest.

'What do you mean, Julia?'

'Nothing.'

'Tell me.'

'All right. Somebody's turned up in my life. Somebody from the past. My godfather, believe it or not. He came to our house the other night. I didn't really want to see him.' Julia's godfather? Phillip's interest sharpened.

Julia was adopted, as he knew very well. Her real parents had died in an accident when she was a baby. She explained. 'He's here on holiday and he looked me up. He brought an album with pictures of my real mother and father and he gave it to me. He knew them before they were married. He was at their wedding.' She gave a shiver. 'But I can't look at the album. I can't bring myself to look at the pictures in it.'

'Why?'

'It's the past and I don't want to reopen it. I've just started to get over the feelings I had about, you know – being adopted.' She rarely said the word. It was a sign of her anxiety. 'I don't want to start looking back.'

'Now who's being weird?' he said, half-teasingly.

'I can't help it. It's the way I feel.'

'Can I see a photo of your real parents?'

'No.'

'You shouldn't deny the past,' he said. As he said it, he felt a twinge of guilt because he remembered what the bird had told him in the dream, how he was guilty of doing the same thing. 'You can't turn away from the past any more than you can live in it. You may have stopped living in the past, but now you are doing something far worse — you are denying the past.'

'I don't want to look at the album; in fact, I don't want to go home knowing it's sitting there waiting for me.'

'What do you want to do?'

'We could go to the park. We could sit under a tree and play a game of chess if you like. I've got my travel set in my satchel.'

Phillip knew better than to pit himself against Julia in a game of chess. The intelligent, clean-faced girl had a mind like a printed circuit when it came to board games, any games. She was still the unbeaten state junior chess champion.

'No thanks,' he said. She looked disappointed. He relented and came up with another suggestion. 'We could stop for a game at the corner store if you want. They've put in a new video game machine, although I should warn you it's a boys' game with machine guns and commandoes and I've played it before, so I'll have an edge on you.'

'I don't mind,' Julia said. 'I'll soon pick it up.' She smiled brightly and confidently. He didn't like that smile.

Only an idiot played games against Julia.

2

The vanishing past

IT WAS LATE AFTERNOON when Phillip arrived home. He thumped up the stairs to his bedroom and dropped his school case disgustedly on the bed. Julia had won almost every game — a war game where players had to fire at an invasion of enemy paratroopers who were dropping out of the sky with their guns blazing.

He turned to sweep his bedroom in a glance, frowning.

Something was missing at home.

What was it? Everything was there; his shelves of books, his portable television set, his wall map of ancient Egypt that showed the thin green river Nile running through the brown desert like a stalk and opening up in the delta region like the green head of a lotus blossom — a journey he used to dream about making.

His parents were missing. They were out. No, it wasn't that. He knew about that. They had told him they were going shopping. They were going away on a trip the next day and they needed to buy a few things before they left. It was something else. What?

Dogstar. That was it. Dogstar hadn't come to greet him. He felt guilty for not noticing straight away.

'Dogstar, where are you, boy?' he called.

He listened for the beat of the dog's paws speeding up the stairs. No dog. Phillip called out again. He went downstairs into the empty kitchen. He slid open the back kitchen door and found Dogstar lying on the concrete step outside. The dog had ignored his homecoming.

'Well that's great, Dogstar,' he said in a hurt voice. 'Very friendly. Don't you come and say hello any more? You're going to be a fat lot of company when Mum and Dad are away.' The dog lay flat out on its side. It lifted its head a fraction, then gave its long, thin tail a lazy flick the way a bored lion might do. 'Come inside and say hello.'

The dog got reluctantly up and came unsteadily into the kitchen as if still half asleep. 'Buck up, 'Star boy. We're going to need each other for the next few days. We're going to be all alone in the world.'

As he looked at the dog, he remembered how he had needed it once before in that other place. He remembered how the dog had run like a living arrow through the pathways and passages of the ancient Egyptian underworld, guiding the lost group of tomb travellers to safety. He remembered the dog's courage, how it had faced the giant scarab beetle in the labyrinth and risked its own life to save Julia's.

'Don't fade away, 'Star boy. I know I forget about you sometimes and I'm sorry, especially since I know you never forget about me.' He felt guilty then for all the times he forgot about Dogstar, especially the times at school when his mind was on lots of other things and Dogstar's mind was only on him as it lay in the backyard and watched the shadows creep across the lawn and go under the trees and lengthen again till it knew it was time for him to come home from school.

The image of the dog softened and swam in Phillip's vision. This time it was because of some tears in his eyes. 'How about something to eat, old mate?' he said, putting on a cheerful voice as if eating made up for everything. 'What are we going to have?' He opened the freezer compartment at the top of the refrigerator.

Inside he saw frosty packets of steak, chops and sausages, mince, a leg of lamb, a chicken, even a frozen pizza. To Phillip it was a frozen wasteland. 'No food in here,' he said. 'I hope Mum and Dad buy some decent food or we'll starve while they're away.' Next he looked in the refrigerator compartment. He spotted an old roast lamb bone on a plate. Perhaps that would cheer up Dogstar.

'Catch the bone, 'Star boy,' Phillip said in an urgent whisper. He tossed it high in the air.

Dogstar would break out of a dead sleep to catch a flying bone because he was a pharaoh hound, and because he was built for speed and his muscles were spring-loaded for action.

He did it now, taking the bone gracefully in midair before it came down to touch the kitchen floor. But the dog did not want to eat it. The pharaoh hound merely sat with it in its mouth, a glum look on its face. Dogstar knew another trick. 'Okay, throw it away, boy.' The pharaoh hound gave a twist of its head and the bone sailed up in the air. It hit the kitchen floor with a thud where it lay ignored.

Phillip went to the pantry next. His eye ran over rows of cans – baked beans, tuna fish, dogfood and a packet of cornflakes. Ah now, here was real food. He opened a can of beef and gravy dogfood for Dogstar and poured it into a dish. He put it on the floor next to the kitchen counter. Dogstar sniffed and looked up at him apologetically. 'Not hungry, boy? You really want to fade away, don't you?'

Phillip took a clean bowl out of the dishwasher and shook the cereal box over the top of it, releasing a shower of golden sun flakes. Funny, the bowl was always a bit smaller than the amount of cereal you wanted, no matter how big a bowl you chose. He shook some more flakes out of the bag, making a pyramid shape in the bowl, a feat of symmetry and balance that would have delighted the heart of an ancient Egyptian.

He found a carton of milk in the refrigerator and opened it, pouring it into the base of the cornflake pyramid. The cornflake pyramid rose and the edges crumbled onto the counter. He sprinkled some sugar over the pyramid and also over a good area of the counter just to make sure he didn't miss the edges of the bowl.

He didn't bother to sit down, but found a spoon in a drawer and took it to the cornflakes like a spade to a garden. More cornflakes spilled over the edges onto the counter. Why didn't they make bigger bowls?

Real food. He spooned mounds of nutty tasting cornflakes, milk and sugar into his mouth and munched the mixture gratefully. It never quite fitted into your mouth either, he thought, wiping bits from his face. 'Don't leave your cereal bowl lying around when you've finished,' his mother always said. 'Rinse the bowl or the bits go hard and stick and they don't come off in the dishwasher.'

There wouldn't be any bits. He'd eat it all. His spoon scraped the bottom of the bowl and he spooned out the last of the milk.

He wondered how his mother and father would enjoy their trip away from him. He remembered how he used to enjoy going on holidays with them, especially when they went camping. But he was much younger then. It was a long time ago. Yet he missed those times a bit.

His parents tooted the car horn in the driveway when they returned from shopping. Phillip went out to the car and helped his mother and father carry their shopping bags into the kitchen before he escaped upstairs. It was best to keep out of their way or they'd make him unpack.

He decided to listen to some music on his CD player. His parents wouldn't try to call him if he played it good and loud. He flicked through a rack of CDs in his collection. Something with a beat that drowned out everything. He chose a rap group. That'd do nicely.

Out of the corner of his eye he saw Dogstar slink into the bedroom. Its manner caught Phillip's attention. It came in slyly, bent low. Its paws were muddied and it carried a bundle of rags in its jaws. It held the bundle with long teeth of distaste, the edges of its muzzle peeled back to avoid touching it. Phillip shoved the CD back. He knew those rags.

Soil covered the mummy's ancient rust of decay, but Phillip recognised the ibis bird. 'Dogstar, no!'

It was the sacred ibis, the mummified bird that Phillip's uncle William Flanders, the Egyptologist, had given him before he died — the one that had started all the trouble the last time, beginning Phillip's tomb-travelling adventure. Dogstar had buried it in a nearby park. Why had the dog brought it back now?

Phillip's dream of the night before came out of the haze of his memory to hit him like an unseen car. The bird had warned him. Now it was happening. The dog dropped the mummified bird onto the blue rug at Phillip's feet and whined.

'You shouldn't have done it, Dogstar. You've gone and dug up the past! Bad dog!' he said, sternly. 'That's all behind us now.' But it wasn't behind them. It was there, lying on the rug. 'I'm finished with the past. I've learnt my lesson. From now on I live in the here and now.'

Dogstar whined in a pleading way.

'What do you want me to do with it?' Phillip said, exasperated. 'Keep it? I'm not going to. I don't believe in magic, mumbo jumbo and curses and stuff. I believe in other things now. I'll show you where this pile of old rags belongs.' Phillip bent and picked up the mummified bird. It was remarkably light; but then it had been dead and dried since the age of the pyramid builders. Phillip took the bird downstairs to the kitchen. His mother stood at the kitchen counter, unpacking groceries from supermarket bags.

'What's that you've got there, Phillip?' his mother said, spotting the object in his hand.

'Nothing,' he said.

'It looks horrible,' she said. 'Like something the dog dragged in.'

'That's exactly what it is. I'll throw it in the bin,' he said.

She did not recognise the ibis bird. The soil clinging to it disguised the mummy wrappings. It was just as well. She loathed the four-thousand-year-old relic even more than Dogstar. The last time she'd seen it, proudly displayed by Phillip on their living room mantelpiece, she'd screamed.

His mother, a thin, nervy woman, wrinkled her nose. 'Not in my kitchen, thankyou. Throw it in the bin outside, only be careful. There's some broken glass in the bin. I've tried to wrap up the bits in newspaper, but you might still cut yourself if you don't go carefully. Oh, and the garbage truck comes in the morning, so while you're at it, please wheel the bin out to the front yard.'

Linkage. One thing always led to another with parents. Parents, especially mothers, linked everything. Why don't you unpack the dishwasher while you're opening it to take out a clean glass? Instead of lying around in your bedroom, why don't you tidy it? If you're too tired to do your homework, you're too tired to go out with your friends. If you're sitting in the backyard, why don't you water the lawn? If you don't pick up your clothes, I won't do any washing. . .

Phillip took a crumpled supermarket bag off the counter and put the bird inside. He tied a knot in the top of the bag and went out through the kitchen door to a large green tub on wheels. He lifted the swing-lid of the bin.

'Garbage!' he said dismissively as he dropped the bird inside.

Dogstar tried to go in after the bird, jumping up on

its back legs, its front paws scraping the rim of the bin, its sharp nose probing the ripe-smelling odours inside. 'Get out of there,' Phillip said. He let the lid fall. It banged shut, narrowly missing Dogstar's nose. The animal looked offended. 'Sorry, Dogstar, but I did warn you.'

Phillip dragged the trundling tub out to the front of their red-brick double-storey home and left it on the grassy verge, under a jacaranda tree. Dogstar stayed at the back door. When Phillip returned, he found the dog lying on the back step, its head on its paws. It sighed heavily and a quiver ran through its frame.

'C'mon, 'Star boy, brighten up.' He bent to give the animal a pat. It gulped. Its eyes, which in anger could throw sparks like metal pieces on a grinding wheel, looked blankly ahead. Again the dog blurred in Phillip's eyes as though viewed through tears. It was the past coming back, squeezing his feelings again.

He rubbed his eyes with the back of his hand. He mustn't start going back over old ground. Forget it. Forget what had happened. It had happened a long time ago, if it had ever happened at all. Nobody else remembered it, not Julia or Barry Coomber and maybe not even Willard Chase — although he hadn't seen him again since their adventure.

Phillip went back inside.

'I've bought some groceries so you won't starve while we're away,' his mother told him. His mother was going away with his father on a business trip, leaving by air early the next morning. It meant that Phillip would have the house to himself for a few days. He was looking forward to it. He was old enough to take care of himself.

The large figure of his father filled the kitchen doorway. 'What's for dinner, Ruth?'

'I bought a hot roast chicken at the supermarket,' she said. She opened a foil bag and slid a roast chicken onto a plate. It was well roasted, its skin a deep brown colour. It reminded Phillip of the excavated ibis bird.

'Nice looking bird,' his father said in a drooling voice.

Bird. Phillip's stomach soured. Chicken was one thing he couldn't face tonight. 'I'm not hungry,' he said.

'All the more chicken for me,' his father said.

His mother frowned at Phillip. 'Are you all right, Phillip?'

'I'm fine.'

'You're not very observant, are you? Don't you want to ask me about the broken glass in the bin? It's from your bedroom. I heard a big crash in your room today and when I ran upstairs to look I found your picture of the Great Pyramid lying on the floor.

'It had fallen off the wall. Completely smashed, the frame broken and bits of glass scattered everywhere. I must have vacuumed for hours to pick up the bits. I'm surprised you didn't notice that your favourite poster was missing.'

He remembered now. He'd felt something was missing when he'd come home after school, and had thought his only worry was Dogstar's absence. But was there something more? Had he not noticed the picture's absence because he had been trying to push ancient Egypt from his mind?

'Where's my picture now?' Phillip said.

'It's gone.'

'You threw it out?'

'No, it's gone. Broken to pieces.'

'A whole pyramid?' He was puzzled.

She nodded. 'All of it.'

'But. . .'

'Don't argue with your mother,' his father said. 'Start carving the bird, Ruth. I'm starving.'

'The broken glass must have sliced your picture into tiny bits,' she told Phillip, taking a carving knife out of the drawer. She sharpened it on a long knife sharpener and sliced through the brown roasted skin of the chicken breast.

Phillip pictured the knife going through the muddied brown wrappings of the mummified ibis bird. The sour feeling rose higher in his throat. 'There wasn't a single piece of your Great Pyramid left. Odd, really,' she said.

Odd all right. Upsetting, too. He'd always loved the picture. Perhaps he was wrong to have loved it. It wasn't good to keep reminders of the past. It was ancient history and unimportant. He suddenly felt tired. 'I'm going to bed,' he said.

'Don't you want any supper? I was hoping you'd take the chicken bones out to the bin after our meal. I don't want them sitting around in the kitchen where the dog will get them. Mind you, he doesn't seem too interested in food, does he?' she said, eyeing the dog who flopped heavily onto the kitchen floor. 'I noticed he'd left a lamb bone lying on my floor.'

'I'm not hungry,' he said again.

'I'll take the bones out later,' his father said.

'Are you all right, Phillip?'

'Fine. I think I'll watch a bit of TV.'

'Don't you have any homework to do?' his mother said. 'If you can sit up and watch TV you can sit up and do some homework.'

'I don't have any homework.'

'None at all?'

'Just some ancient Egyptian stuff to read, but I already know it.'

'You read it,' his father said.

'I don't have to. We're going on an excursion tomorrow to the national museum. I'm going to see it all in the museum anyway.'

'Good. I'm glad you're having an excursion to the museum. That'll be nice for you, Phillip. You love the museum, don't you, especially the ancient Egyptian section.'

'Not really.'

'You've changed,' his mother said. Mothers were suspicious of any change.

'You used to drive us mad with ancient Egypt,' his father complained.

'It just doesn't matter to me any more.'

He hadn't told them what had happened. They had always found his love of ancient Egypt and its mysteries a source of concern. It wasn't a healthy preoccupation for a young boy, they said. And now they were concerned because he was changing. You could never satisfy parents, Phillip decided.

'You're not quite yourself are you, Phillip? Perhaps an early night will do you good,' his mother said. 'We're leaving early in the morning for the airport, so in case you're in the shower or something and we don't say a proper goodbye, give your mother a kiss goodbye.'

She turned her thin cheek and he dutifully pecked it.

'Look after the house, son,' his father said with awkward affection, thumping Phillip's shoulder. 'No mad teenage parties while we're away, do you hear?'

'Fine Dad. Enjoy your trip,' Phillip said. Suddenly he wished he were going somewhere, too. He trudged up the stairs to his bedroom. Dogstar did not follow him to bed.

That was odd, too.

He switched on a small television set in his bedroom. What was on? News by the look of it. A picture of a woman announcer at a news desk slid onto the screen. It was a satellite news report from overseas.

'And in the United States today, ancient Egyptian tomb treasures mysteriously vanish.' The camera cut away to a view of a gleaming gold sarcophagus in a display case, along with winking pieces of ancient Egyptian jewellery and tomb furniture. The picture then dissolved to the same case which was now yawningly empty.

'Modern day tomb robbers struck at a museum in Boston,' the announcer continued the story. 'Fabulous tomb treasures, part of an exhibition currently touring the United States, have disappeared. The treasures, on loan from the Cairo museum, are indemnified by the US government. However, experts are saying the pieces are priceless.

'This follows a similar disappearance in Paris last week of objects from an Egyptian exhibition of tomb treasures. International antiquity experts and police, who have seen a spate of such disappearances, are at a loss to explain the mysteries.'

The camera cut to a baffled-looking museum curator. 'It was as if the collection of guarded treasures just flew away,' the man said, spreading his hands. 'We don't know how — or who is responsible.'

Depressing, Phillip thought. He switched off the TV set before going to bed. Imagine all of Egypt's treasures simply vanishing.

He looked at the blank spot on the wall where the picture of the Great Pyramid had been, a paler square than the rest of the wall around it. The nail was still in the wall. Why had the picture fallen and how had the scene of the pyramid disappeared?

He swiched off his bedside lamp and went to sleep, dreaming of Egypt disappearing. Dogstar faded in and out of his dreams.

3

Robbers of the past

SOMETHING IN THE STREET below was pulsing with light, throwing shadows on his bedroom wall.

It woke him. His eyes, still trying to shed sleep, focussed on a large shadow on the bedroom wall that detached itself from the rest. He recognised the outline of a bird. The shape fell exactly on the spot where his pyramid picture had been.

Phillip twisted to look at the window.

He saw a massive bird perched on his window sill, lit by the glow from outside. It was looking at him. Phillip took the shock of maliciously gleaming eyes, eyes that were not bird's eyes, in a head that was not a bird's head.

It was a small, wig-surrounded human face with painted eyes in the ancient Egyptian style and a wispy curling beard on its chin. He sat up. The bird flapped away into the darkness.

A soul bird.

Here?

Phillip felt his own heart beat as wildly as a bird's. Where was Dogstar? Phillip searched the eerily glowing room. 'Dogstar?' Was the animal asleep under the bed? He listened. No sound of stirring. That was unusual. He snapped on the light.

There wasn't much of Dogstar left on the blue bedroom rug, just a leather collar that carried a circular municipal dog tag, a strip of plastic clipped on the leather and bearing a registration number.

Phillip picked up the collar. It hadn't come undone. The buckle was closed. Had it slipped over the dog's head? He looked at the small leather loop in his hands. It was hard to believe that a dog the size of Dogstar had ever worn it, let alone slipped out of it, even though the aristocratic running hound had a remarkably slender, tapered neck and even though the animal was thinner than usual. The disappearance left only one possibility and that was an impossibility.

The dog had vanished.

Phillip swallowed. Things were closing in on him the way they had done once before. He went to the window. It was a grey misty morning. He discovered the source of the pulsing light in his room. It came from the green garbage bin that sat on the grassy verge of the street below the house, partly hidden by the jacaranda tree. A phosphorescent glow pulsed through the thick, opaque plastic.

How was it possible? Was it the streetlight playing tricks as it filtered through the jacaranda leaves? Maybe the leaves were stirring in a breeze and making the light come and go. He peered into the outstretched branches of the jacaranda tree. Not a leaf stirred. There was no breeze.

It was the ibis bird — calling to him. Why? There was only one explanation. It wanted to be released from the bin.

Phillip looked at his wristwatch. It was 7.30 in the morning. The garbage truck would arrive at any minute to collect the garbage in the bin and when that happened, the ibis bird, along with the week's garbage, would go to the council tip to be buried forever. The bird knew it. It did not want to end up under tonnes of rotting garbage.

Phillip dragged on a pair of jeans and T-shirt over his lean body and slipped on some sneakers over bare feet and, as an afterthought, pocketed Dogstar's collar. Too late, he heard the rumble of a garbage truck approaching. He ran down the stairs, half tripping over the trailing laces of his untied sneakers. He unlocked the front door and wrenched it open.

He saw a blue-singleted garbage collector dressed like a jogger dragging the green bin off the grassy verge to the back of the rumbling, stationary truck.

'No, wait!' Phillip shouted.

The man hardly threw a glance at Phillip before turning his back. 'Sorry, mate! If you've got any more rubbish, it'll have to wait till next time!' The garbage collector hooked the green bin to the back of the garbage truck. Hydraulics whined, and the bin rose off the ground and the rubbish tipped smoothly into an iron mouth. Metallic planes like the palpus flaps around an insect's mouth devoured the packets and bags, boxes and clippings that spilled towards it, taking it all hungrily into an iron stomach. The stomach rumbled with satisfaction.

The bird was gone.

Phillip felt limp with helplessness. He saw his stupidity now. Throwing out the bird had been a mistake. Dogstar had brought the bird back for a reason. It had overcome its dislike of the ibis bird in order to tell him something.

An image of Dogstar filled his mind, an image blurred as if seen through tears. The image slipped away.

The ibis bird was a part of what was happening. He felt it with certainty. He did not know how he was going to get Dogstar back, but as a first step he knew that he would have to recover the ibis bird.

The garbage man lowered Phillip's empty bin, released it and swung it back onto the verge; he gave a call, signalling the driver to proceed and the truck rumbled on to the next house, the last one in the street.

Phillip came to a decision. If he had dared to travel into the forbidden underworld to rescue a loved one, then he would not be afraid to visit a garbage tip. He'd follow the truck to the tip and try to get his ibis bird back.

Phillip went to the garage to fetch his bicycle. Good, the headlamp was on the bike. It was misty and he would need it. The bicycle helmet was nearby on a shelf. He jammed the helmet over his uncombed fair hair. He turned on the bicycle lamp and wheeled the bike past his father's car, swung himself onto the saddle and pedalled into the street, following the truck which had finished its run and was now going back to the council tip.

A land cruiser came towards Phillip from the other direction, its headlights momentarily blinding him. It braked suddenly as it drew level.

'Phillip!' He thought he heard a muffled cry. He glimpsed a man's face under a battered hat, pressed to the glass of the wound-up window.

No, it couldn't be him, not him.

Phillip kept pedalling.

He followed the garbage truck to the council tip which lay about five kilometres away from his house. In the cool, face-scrubbing air of early morning, vaguely shaped fears whipped past the edges of Phillip's mind like the passing scenery of houses that thinned out and gave way to more trees as he drew closer to the tip.

He came to a high red-brick wall that surrounded the tip. The tip had once been a brickworks site. Trucks and cars bringing garbage to the tip had to go through gates manned by an attendant in a booth who charged private vehicles a fee according to their loads. Even at this time of the morning, people were arriving with loads of rubbish, garden cuttings and junk in trailers.

How would Phillip get in? The attendant would not let him walk through the gate. Up ahead the garbage truck rumbled through a separate gate. He had to follow it quickly or lose sight of where it dumped its load. Phillip saw a station wagon pull up behind a queue of other vehicles at a gate. It towed a trailer filled with tree branches and garden clippings.

It gave him an idea. He could smuggle himself aboard the trailer. First, he hid his bike in some bushes beside the red-brick wall and then, bending low, he approached the station wagon and trailer from behind. In the cool morning air, steam from the vehicle's exhaust blurred the driver's view of the back.

Phillip looked for a good spot to jump in. He found an opening under some cut branches. That would do.

He slipped into the trailer, covering himself with the branches and with smaller garden clippings. The trailer smelled dryly of withering vegetation. The engine rumbled, the trailer lurched and they moved forward. They stopped at the gateway. Would the attendant search the trailer?

Phillip imagined himself as a prisoner of war in an escape movie, attempting to break out of a prison camp — except he wasn't breaking out, he was breaking in. Had anyone ever bothered to smuggle themselves into a rubbish dump before? he wondered. He pictured a blade flashing by his startled eyes as an armed guard probed the garden refuse with the point of a bayonet, searching for escapees. Hurry up, he willed the driver.

The garbage truck was getting away, the rumble of its engine receding in the distance. The driver of the station wagon revved his engine. They trundled into the tip, going along a bumpy dirt road. The sour-ripe smell of the rubbish dump seeped into the trailer to reach Phillip, making his nostrils flare. They slowed, stopped. They must have caught up with a vehicle in front.

Hurry up. Where was the garbage truck now? He couldn't hear it any more. It was drowned out by the high-revving clangour of some heavy mechanical equipment at work. He'd better come out for a look. He sat up, pushing off a blanket of clippings and cut branches.

He'd expected a city refuse tip to be a desolate place, a scene of abandonment, but he was surprised. Although pyramids of rubbish rose around him, the scene had the productive air of a construction site. Vehicles, some with trailers, roamed about like busy insects.

A couple of yellow Caterpillar graders were busily ploughing the rubbish into areas and covering them with dirt. They were working on a series of levels, filling the site systematically. Phillip looked around for the bulky shape of a garbage truck. His eye settled on one, then on another and another. He groaned. A fleet of trucks, all identical, stood in a row, spilling the regurgitated waste of the suburbs onto the ground.

How would he find the bird now? How would he ever learn what had become of Dogstar?

'Sorry 'Star boy,' he said under his breath. 'I've messed it up this time.'

He swung a leg over the side of the trailer and jumped out, walking numbly across a clearing towards the row of garbage trucks, avoiding some deep, criss-crossed hollows left by caterpillar wheels in the red clay soil. He sat on a drum. His sneaker shoelaces were still undone, he saw, looking down. He bent to tie them.

A four-wheel-drive growled by, paused and turned to pull up with a squeak of brakes in front of him, spilling light into his eyes. He shielded his eyes. 'Don't do that,' he said irritably. The driver killed the engine and the lights and climbed out. He walked towards Phillip.

'You look down in the dumps, kid,' a familiar, joking voice said to him.

'That's not funny,' Phillip said. A passing car lit the rugged face of a man with broad, calm eyes beneath a battered hat.

'Willard Chase!' He was dressed for an archaeological expedition in khaki gear. What was he doing here? He stopped in front of Phillip and held out a hand. It *was* him. Phillip grabbed Willard's hand like a drowning boy and his arm tingled as if voltage ran down it. He was back in an adventure. He knew it now.

'What's happening, Phillip?'

'The past has caught up with me again,' Phillip said. 'That awful, scary past.'

'It's caught up with both of us.' Willard looked around. 'This place reminds me of it. Remember the foul-smelling labyrinth where the giant scarab beetle lived, the demented creature that ran around like a locomotive, rolling a giant ball of dung like a black sun and squashing people?'

'Do you think I could ever forget?'

'What are you doing here at this hour of the morning?'

'What are you doing here?'

'I followed you from your home. I planned to have a chat with you and maybe offer you a ride to school.'

'I'm here to find a bird.'

'In a garbage dump?' Willard Chase looked amused. 'What kind of bird?'

'A four-thousand-year-old mummified ibis bird.'

'This is obviously some new branch of archaeology I don't know about,' the archaeological detective said dryly.

'It's the magical ibis bird Uncle William gave me. I did a stupid thing. I threw the ibis bird in our bin and the garbage truck collected it and brought it here. I've changed my mind and want it back. Dogstar's gone missing and I think the ibis bird's got something to do with it.'

'Dogstar's gone?' Phillip took the collar out of his pocket and showed him.

'Just vanished,' Phillip said. 'I can't explain it.'

Willard Chase rested a large desert boot on the drum beside him. 'Maybe I can explain it. But first tell me everything that's happened.'

Phillip told him and Willard Chase nodded as he spoke, hardly looking surprised about anything he said, even about the soul bird appearing at the bedroom window. 'Why is this happening again?' Phillip said, searching the man's face for an answer.

Willard Chase raised his hat a bit to scratch his forehead thoughtfully. 'I don't want you to blame yourself, Phillip, but I think it's because of something you did on our previous journey. Do you remember that scroll of the *Book of the Dead* that you left behind in the underworld, the one your Uncle William had buried with him when he died, like an Egyptian of old? Well, as we both discovered, that particular scroll was not only a magical passport to the Egyptian underworld; it was also a map – showing the way to and from that world. We used the map to find our way out last time. Unfortunately, you left the scroll there and now something is using it to reach this world.'

'Something?'

'Take a look up there. Those aren't pigeons.'

Phillip turned his eyes to the sky. The mist was clearing. There were dark birds planing in circles above the tip. 'Soul birds,' Willard Chase said. 'The underworld has come to take back what belongs to Egypt.'

The sun was beginning to rise above the pyramids of refuse, bathing the scene in gold. It looked quite beautiful, Phillip thought. How could a rubbish tip look beautiful? 'The underworld has taken Dogstar, too,' Willard said.

'I don't believe it. Why?'

'Partly to be spiteful because they resented your invasion of their secret realm. But more importantly because your dog is a pharaoh hound, a breed from ancient Egypt. They want Egypt's past back — *all* of it. Amazing as it sounds, Phillip, Egypt is disappearing. Fading away in front of our eyes.

'Treasures taken from the tombs are vanishing. Statues of pharaohs are crumbling into dust. Temples like Luxor and Karnak are splitting and toppling. Blocks of limestone are crashing down off the Great Pyramid. Cleopatra's needle fell off the Thames Embankment in London. Nefertiti's elegant head has toppled off its long neck in Berlin. Mummies are vanishing from museum cases. Papyrus is crumbling into dust. And worse.'

'Worse?'

'Egypt is taking back her history. Biblical scholars are astounded. Mention of Egypt has actually been obliterated from editions of the Bible. Whole pages have vanished, whole passages mysteriously erased. Check a copy of the Bible yourself and you'll see. No Joseph in Egypt, no Moses, no Exodus, no promised land. . . you can fill in the blanks.

'And there's more. Egypt's legacy is vanishing. *Paper*. The word itself, as you know, comes from *papyrus*, an Egyptian invention. There's never been a disaster like it. It's a closely kept secret, but books in the the Library of Congress in the United States are turning to dust.

'Officially the building is closed for renovations, but that's only a cover. Inside, it looks as if a dust storm has hit the place. Books turning to powder everywhere. The same dust storm is blowing through libraries around the world. Do you know what this means? All the printed knowledge of the world will vanish if we don't stop them.'

'But how can we stop them?'

Willard Chase shrugged. 'This is the biggest archaeological detective puzzle in history, kid — and, although it's my specialty, I don't know which way to turn. I hoped you could suggest something. You were pretty useful last time.'

Not knowing which way to turn wasn't unusual for Willard Chase, Phillip remembered, feeling a bit superior. The archaeological detective was smart at solving archaeological puzzles, digging up artefacts from thieves who stole them and buried them a second time in the modern day underworld of crime, but for a man who spent his time crawling around passages and dark places sifting through layers of conspiracy, treachery and greed, he had a poorly developed sense of direction.

'We have to go back to find out what's happening and try to stop them, to get the scroll back or at least destroy it,' Willard said. 'That's all I know.'

'I don't want to go back there,' Phillip said. 'It's not right. I've learnt my lesson. We should live in the here and now and not chase after the past.'

'If Egypt steals back its past, Phillip, there'll be no here and now. There'll be no future. Do you know how much our civilisation owes ancient Egypt? Pick any field you like. *Architecture*? Egypt was the first great builder in stone. Will our public buildings disappear? *Medicine*? The Greeks say they learnt it all from ancient Egypt.

'There is a medical papyrus that deals with the treatment of a sword wound. It prescribes the application of a fungus taken from the underside of a lily. *Penicillin* — three thousand years ago! Will antibiotics disappear? The Egyptians invented the first civilised *calendar*. They divided the day and night into twelve hours each. Will our time disappear? They invented the world's first *nationstate*. Will the nations of the world disintegrate?'

'If it was true and I did go back — and I'm not saying I would — then it would only be for one reason and not for the reasons you say. I want my dog back. That would be my only reason for going. I couldn't care less about the past. If the underworld wants to steal back Egypt's past, it can have it. The past belongs to the dead anyway.'

'No, it doesn't,' Willard Chase said heatedly. 'The past belongs to everyone. It belongs to you and me.'

'Dogstar belongs to me,' Phillip said grittily. 'That's all I need to know. They're not having my dog. Dogstar led us through the underworld once and I owe my life to Dogstar.'

'There's still the small question of getting back there.'

'You managed it last time. How did you do it?'

Willard looked sheepish. 'I don't exactly know. It may surprise you, but I had lost my way and stumbled into the wrong passage. I've tried to find the passage since, but can't!'

'Then if we did go, we'd have to go my way. We'd have to do it the same way as last time.'

'That's what I hoped you'd say. That's why I've come to you. You're my last hope.'

'The magical ibis bird is the key,' Phillip said. 'It

sparked the journey last time. We'll have to find it.'
He checked on the garbage trucks. The trucks had
dumped their loads of rubbish and were leaving in a
convoy along the dirt road that led out of the tip. 'We'll
have to do a bit of scratching around though, I'm
afraid. The ibis bird is buried in one of those piles of
rubbish over there.'

He went to the base of the first mountain of garbage.
Willard followed. 'I'll start on this one. You take the
next.'

Willard Chase smiled. 'Anything you say. This is
your archaeological dig.'

They began to scratch.

'What am I looking for?' Willard said.

'A green plastic garbage bag.'

'Green,' Willard said, unenthusiastically. 'Couldn't it
be a purple one or a pink one? They're all green.
There must be more green bags piled up here than
stone blocks in the Great Pyramid.' It was an exaggera-
tion, but only a slight one. They began tearing open
green bags. 'What am I looking for inside the green
bags?'

'A white grocery bag.'

'White grocery bag,' he said resignedly. It wasn't
making their job any easier. Willard tore open a bag,
chatting as he worked. 'I've been on a lot of archaeological digs in my time, but never one quite like
this. You know, five hundred years from now this stuff
will probably fascinate some archaeologist.' He kicked
a few plastic liquid detergent bottles aside.

'What will it tell him about us? Maybe he'll con-
clude we were hooked on eternity like the ancient
Egyptians. Take these plastic bottles, for example.

We're supposed to be a throwaway society, yet this packaging is made to last for eternity. Non-degradable. Designed to last longer than Egypt's mummies.'

Phillip ripped open a plastic bag. The sour-ripe smell of the air turned sickly sweet. Rotting fruit slid out like furry animals. Flies swarmed, even at this early hour.

'What does the bird look like?'

'Like a mummified ibis bird, all wrapped in bandages and stuff. Only this one's a bit grubby and muddy looking. Dogstar buried it in a park.'

It was a hopeless search and even Phillip's keen efforts soon slackened. He kicked a green bag dejectedly. Household garbage spilled out like a burst belly — cans, packets, a plastic ice-cream container. A doll's head with a broken brow and empty eye sockets poked out.

Phillip wouldn't give up. He went on to the next pile. It was worse than hopeless. But he kept going and so did Willard Chase. By the third pile, Phillip tasted despair. Willard Chase shoved some garbage bags aside with his hand and gave a muffled curse.

'. . .broken glass!'

'Did you say broken glass?'

'I said something worse, but I won't repeat it.'

Phillip reached him in one bound.

'Nice of you to be so concerned,' Willard said, 'but it's just a nick on my finger.'

'You've found it.'

'Found what?' Willard wrapped a handkerchief around his bleeding finger.

'*It!*' Phillip said excitedly. 'The bird. You've put your finger on it!' Phillip carefully split the bag open and drew out a plastic grocery bag. He spread out a soggy newspaper and tipped out the contents of the grocery bag. A pile of gnawed bones dropped onto the newspaper.

Willard Chase craned over him to look. 'It's a bird all right,' he said. 'Or at least it was.' The smell of stale sage and onions rose to greet Phillip's nostrils. 'Roast chicken, I'd say.'

It was the remains of his mother and father's roast chicken dinner.

The sourness he had felt in his stomach that night returned. He fished deeper in the split green bag, pulling out another white grocery bag, this one tied at the top by its handles. The bag was very light, but so was Phillip's heart, because he knew that he had found it.

Phillip untied the handles of the bag and drew out the mummified ibis bird.

'Got you,' Phillip said, smiling broadly at the bundle of rags.

'Looks pretty ancient,' Willard Chase said. 'Old Kingdom, judging by the wrappings. Imagine an archaeologist of the future finding an Egyptian mummified ibis in a municipal tip! That would fox him!'

'It's four thousand years old and rich in magical significance. Uncle William told me.'

'We could do with some magic. How about making a wish?'

Phillip looked at his wristwatch. 'Okay, I wish you'd drive me home. I don't want to be late for school. But first I must pick up my bike. I left it in the bushes outside the tip.'

Phillip climbed into the land cruiser beside Willard Chase and they drove out of the tip to collect his bike.

4

The excursion

HIS RESCUE MISSION TO THE TIP had taken him longer than he thought. He found a note from his mother waiting on the kitchen counter.

Dear Phillip:

Sorry we missed you, but glad you've started taking Dogstar on your morning bike ride again. He needs the exercise. He's been looking a bit peaky lately and, as I said, not eating too well. Look after him and yourself. See you both eat well while we're away.

Love, Mum & Dad.

While Willard went to a downstairs bathroom to clean his cut finger, Phillip went upstairs to shower away the grime of the garbage tip. He dressed for school, slipping Dogstar's collar into his pocket. 'I'm going to carry it with me until the day I can put it back around your neck, Dogstar,' he vowed silently.

When he came downstairs, he found Willard Chase in their living room examining a row of books in their bookcase. Willard extended a long finger, freshly wrapped in elastoplast, to pull out the family Bible.

'Try reading this,' he said.

'I don't want to,' Phillip said. 'It's ancient history.'

The archaeologist had a purposeful light in his eye. 'Take it and page through to Exodus. I want to prove something to you.'

Phillip took the Bible from him and opened it, paging through the volume to the front. He never reached Exodus. A trickle of dust like the fine sand in an hourglass fell out of the bottom of the book and spilled onto his shoes. He snapped the book shut as if to protect what remained of history, sending a cloud of dust into his face.

'So it's an old book,' Phillip said, coughing. 'I told you it's ancient history.'

'Egypt is disappearing, Phillip. You've got to believe it.'

'Well, I don't. Will you drop me off at school now?'

'Sure, and I'll pick you up afterwards.'

The school group, led by Mr Patrick, swarmed up the steps of the national museum building. Phillip glanced up at the sky above the columned building. The weather had changed. It had become a dull, overcast day and rain threatened. Phillip almost tripped on the next step.

He noticed a large dark bird sitting high on the parapet of the museum building, bending over the edge to look down at them. The bird did not have a beak-face, but a pale, oval-shaped face like a human face. An owl? In the daytime? The eyes that looked down were bright and malicious.

A soul bird.

He flashed anger at the bird. Did it know where Dogstar had gone? He remembered how soul birds had tried to steal the animal in that underworld place of gateways and passageways. . .

*   *   *

The ceiling rose in the passage until it was lost in gloom over their heads. Something passed low over Phillip's head, brushing his hair. Was it a bat? He thought he heard the whistle of birds' wings.

'What was that?' Coomber said as another flitted past his ear. Phillip looked up. A winged creature sailed over his head and he almost stumbled when he saw a downturned human face on the bird, a small, Egyptian face with a beard and painted eyes. Then it was gone.

Had he imagined it? More birds swooped. He noticed a ledge running along the top of the passage just before it disappeared into darkness. Birds settled on the ledge to watch them go by. Another bird swooped low, its wingtips brushing Phillip's ear.

'Go, false shades who do not belong!' it said. It gave a piping laugh as it climbed into the blackness.

'Ba birds,' Uncle William said uneasily. 'Soul birds with vulture's bodies and human heads. Watch out for their claws and ignore what they say. They can be spiteful to the living and quite malignant.'

One dived too close to Dogstar who snapped its jaws and took a few feathers out of its wing, making it crash-land further down the passage. It got up and hopped grotesquely on the floor. Dogstar broke free from Phillip and ran after it.

'Leave it, Dogstar,' Phillip shouted after it. 'Here, boy!'

The soul birds sitting on the ledge above picked up his cry and parroted his words. They mimicked Phillip's voice perfectly, although at a higher pitch. 'Leave it, Dogstar! Leave it, Dogstar! Here, boy! There, boy! Here, boy!'

Dogstar twisted its head around in confusion. The injured bird made a run before achieving a wobbly take- off. 'Here, boy! There, boy! Here, there, and everywhere, boy!'

Dogstar yelped and ran around in circles, baffled. They dive-bombed it, calling out its name, streaking off down the passage. 'Here boy! Here, boy!' Dogstar snapped at the flitting missiles. The shrill cry of its name ran in spiralling echoes down the passage. Dogstar took off after the sound.

'Dogstar! Here, boy!' Phillip shouted after it, but it was just one more sound to confuse the dog.

The tomb travellers broke into a run. Phillip expected to find Dogstar around every turn of the passage, but empty passage after empty passage flung its disappointing length ahead of him.

*   *   *

Remembering, he felt a deeper pang of loss.

Where was Dogstar now? 'I'll get my dog back from you; I don't know how, but I will,' he telegraphed a silent promise to the bird on the museum's roof.

His eyes were still on the bird when somebody gave him a shove from behind. His foot caught the edge of a step and he tumbled, dropping a clipboard and a pen he'd been carrying. 'Look where you're going,' somebody said, stepping quickly past Coomber.

Phillip picked himself up. Barry Coomber gave Phillip a smirk as he went ahead, falling in beside Mr

Patrick for protection. Julia came to Phillip's aid. She picked up Phillip's clipboard, while Phillip made a grab between trampling feet for his pen. He nearly had his fingers squashed.

'He'll keep!' Julia said angrily.

'Forget it.'

'Come along, you two,' Mr Patrick called to them. 'Stop dragging your feet.'

'Are you all right, Phillip?' Julia said, continuing up the steps with him. 'You've gone white.'

Soul bird, Phillip thought. It was a warning. Why was it here at the museum? He wondered what surprises lay in store for him here.

'I'm fine. It's Dogstar. He's gone,' he whispered to Julia.

'Gone where?'

'Missing.'

'He's run away?'

'He's been taken.'

'What makes you say that?'

'This.' Phillip dug into a pocket and took out Dog-star's collar. 'Somebody took it off the dog and left it behind to tell me. The dog couldn't have got out of it. I'm not going to rest until I put it back around Dogstar's neck.'

'I'm sure he's just wandering in the neighbourhood.'

'He's gone, Julia.'

'I'll help you look for him.'

'It's no use; he can't be found.'

'He can't have vanished off the planet.'

'I wish I could be sure of that,' he said in a mysterious voice.

'Don't say silly things. He'll turn up.'

'Maybe,' Phillip said, 'but where?'

The school group followed the signs to the Egyptian rooms on a higher level. Mr Patrick reached the Egyptian section first. He went to the head of a long, low, body-length glass case that stood in the centre of the room and he signalled the class to gather round. 'Who'd like to tell me about this exhibit and about the rituals and beliefs it demonstrates?' he said.

'Not much to tell,' Barry Coomber said, pressing his face to the case and making marks on the glass. 'Pretty empty display case, if you ask me.'

'Thankyou, Coomber.' Mr Patrick turned wearily to Phillip. 'Come to our aid, will you, Phillip Simpson. Tell the class about this exhibit.'

Phillip stared into the dimly lit case. He glimpsed his reflection in the glass. He saw his own eyes, blue, faraway-looking eyes, staring back at him. He saw surprise jump into those eyes. He felt a giddiness suck at him as if he were looking over the edge of a high building. The mummy was gone. The case was empty. Phillip began to believe.

Phillip came through the school gate alone. Julia stayed behind to attend a chess club meeting. Phillip found Willard Chase waiting for him in his land cruiser.

'It's true,' Phillip said, climbing into the land cruiser beside him. 'Egypt is vanishing. The mummy in the museum had disappeared. And I saw a soul bird sitting on top of the building.'

'I don't know how much time we've got left. We'll have to do something pretty quickly.'

Phillip thought about it on the way home. What had

made the journey happen last time? Sleep. He had been asleep. That was it.

'We'll have to go to sleep,' Phillip told Willard Chase. He went into the house with Willard following, and threw his school case onto a living room chair.

Willard Chase looked surprised. 'I know you were up early this morning — but do you really want a nap?'

'We have to go to sleep in order to go there. That's what happened last time.'

'You sure?'

'Positive.'

'Suits me.' Willard stretched out gratefully on a couch. He tipped his battered hat over his eyes. 'I was up early, too.'

Phillip curled up in a chair. He thought sleep wouldn't come because when his eyes closed he saw the frieze of running figures again. Like an outside observer he saw himself, Julia, Barry Coomber and Willard running through passages in the underworld, searching for Dogstar. 'Hang on boy, I'll come to you — if there's any way on earth. Or beyond it.' To his surprise, sleep came easily. A crash of thunder woke him up. Willard Chase did not stir. Phillip looked at his watch. It was five-thirty and nearly dark.

It hadn't worked. Why?

Everything was the same, even the storm.

Then he remembered. Things weren't quite the same. Two people were missing. Julia and Barry Coomber. For some reason Julia and Coomber had been part of it last time and maybe they had to be part of it again.

'It won't work with just the two of us,' he said emphatically.

Willard Chase gave a grunt and raised the brim of his hat. 'Are we there? Hardly felt us land.'

'We're getting nowhere. We must have Julia and Barry Coomber here, too.'

Willard made a face. 'You really want that bully-boy tagging along again?'

'Not especially, but without him we're not going to get there. Don't you see? For some reason he's part of it. So's Julia. I'll have to get them to join us.' He thought quickly. What would be the sure way to attract Julia? 'I know,' he said. 'I'll invite Julia to come and play a board game.' Nothing would stop Julia coming over if he promised to play a board game. 'That will do it. She loves games.'

'I haven't forgotten,' Willard said. 'Julia's skills came in very handy when she challenged the great ape to the senet match. It was the greatest board game I ever watched.'

'Coomber's going to be more difficult. He's not exactly my best friend and he'll be suspicious if I invite him over.'

'You could ask for his help.'

'Barry Coomber's not the most helpful kid in the world.'

'No. I seem to remember he was a pretty grasping kid. Use some bait.'

Phillip called Julia first. 'I knew you'd call,' Julia said. 'I was thinking of you.'

'Can you come over, Jool?'

'No, I've got an ancient Egyptian assignment to do. So have you,' she reminded him. 'It's due on Monday.'

'I couldn't care less about assignments.'

'You will on Monday.'

'I want you to come here now.'

Interest stirred in the voice on the line. 'What's wrong, Phillip? You're beginning to act strangely again, the way you did once before.'

'I want a chance to get even for the video game yesterday. How about a game of chess?' It didn't matter which game he chose — draughts, Trivial Pursuit, chess; it would turn out the same way. Julia would cut him into little pieces.

'You're challenging me to a game of chess!' Curiosity sat up in her voice.

'If you're up to it.'

That startled Julia. 'Something is wrong. Sorry, I didn't realise quite how wrong. I'll come right over.' The phone clicked and the line went dead in Phillip's ear.

Now there were three tomb travellers. One more to go. He rang Barry Coomber's number. The phone was answered by his surly big brother Terry.

'Yeah?'

'Is that Midnight Spares?' Phillip was tempted to ask, but he decided against it and politely asked to speak to Barry instead.

'Wait,' Terry told Phillip brusquely and called out to his younger brother. 'It's that weird kid Phillip Simpson.' Barry Coomber came to the phone. 'Yeah?' he said in the same hostile tone as his brother.

Phillip pictured the hefty boy with shiny, bullying eyes. 'It's Phillip.'

'So?'

'My parents are away and I'm getting rid of some

stuff. Selling it cheap.'

'What sort of stuff?'

'Computer games, some CDs, that sort of thing.'

'When?'

'Right now. But you'd better hurry. I'm giving the stuff away.'

'Yeah well okay, but only if you're giving. . .' He put down the phone.

'Now we wait,' Phillip said.

'I'm looking forward to seeing Julia again,' Willard said, 'but I'm not so sure about Barry Coomber even though he did prove to be pretty resourceful when he was cornered.'

'Slippery is a better word.'

'How are the pair of them?'

'Much the same as before. They never remembered what happened. It was as if it never happened. I thought you'd forgotten it, too.'

'I wish I had.'

Julia, who lived only a few houses away, was first to arrive. Phillip answered the door and let her in. It had started to rain. There were raindrops on her red blouse and blue jeans. She carried a fold-up portable chessboard and a box of chess pieces under her arm. She smiled at him brightly. 'Hi, Phillip. You asked for this!'

As she walked inside she caught sight of Willard Chase on the couch and the smile slid off her face. 'Oh no.' She dropped the chess box, and wooden pawns, knights, bishops, kings and queens scattered across the wooden floorboards like an army in disarray.

Willard apologised. 'Hi, Julia. Sorry the sight of me throws such a scare into you.' He smiled, getting up to greet her. 'It's good to see you again.'

He held out his hand and she shook it limply. 'Willard,' she said mechanically as if placing him like a chess piece on the board of her brain. Her eyes turned anxiously to Phillip. 'You're not going to scare me again, are you Phillip? That's what you did last time. I came over one night to play a game with you and ended up playing a role in a nightmare.'

'You remember it?'

'I do now. But I didn't until this morning. I woke up having dreams, dreams of what happened with the five of us.' She touched the side of her forehead. 'I woke up remembering things that I didn't know I knew.'

'It's started again, Julia.'

'Why?'

'We've all got to go back there.'

'Oh no.' She bent to pick up the chess pieces. Phillip and Willard helped her. Her hand was trembling as she dropped a black bishop into the wooden box.

'You told a fib to get me here,' Julia said reproachfully when they had picked up all the pieces and had sat down. 'Now you owe me the truth.'

He told her about Dogstar and about Egypt disappearing and proved it by showing her the Bible. The deterioration was getting worse. The whole book was turning to sand. 'The inventors of paper are stealing back their invention,' Willard said. That worried the bookish Julia almost as much as Dogstar going missing, even though she loved the dog who had once saved her life.

'Lovely Dogstar! What can we do for him?'

'Go back for him, but first we need Coomber.'

'Not him too!'

Willard Chase smiled. 'Julia and I see things the same way.'

'I know how you feel about him,' Phillip said. 'I feel the same way, but he's part of the team. The team must be complete or at least as complete as we can make it without Dogstar.'

They turned their heads at the sound of an abrupt rap at the front door. 'That's Barry,' Phillip said. 'I don't want to scare him off. You two had better hide in the next room until I get a chance to settle him down. If he spots Willard, he won't stop running.'

They nodded understandingly and withdrew to the adjoining dining room.

Phillip opened the front door. Barry Coomber stood in the doorway looking wet and ugly. He scowled at Phillip. 'This had better be worth getting wet for or you're going to walk home with me in the rain. Where's the stuff you're giving away?'

'In the lounge.' Coomber pushed past Phillip to go inside, leaving wet pools on the floor of the hallway. Phillip deadlocked the door after him and secretly pocketed the key. Coomber reached the centre of the room and his eyes searched for the CDs and computer games Phillip had promised. He noticed Julia's chess board and the box of chessmen on a table.

'I've invited a few friends over to meet you,' Phillip said. He called out to the two waiting in the dining room. 'You can come out now.'

Willard Chase and Julia walked into the room. Barry Coomber's aggression evaporated at the sight of Willard. 'Oh no, you don't. I know what's happening all of a sudden. You sickos aren't dragging me back there again. I'm out of here. See you around.'

Thunder rumbled overhead. Lightning cracked like a broken power cable at a window. It whiplashed across the room, freezing them like a photographic image on film. The jagged spear of light struck the mantelpiece where the mummified ibis bird sat, throwing off a shower of sparks.

Phillip, Coomber, Julia and Willard Chase became fixed like figures in a frozen tableau. The tableau wheeled, began to climb and, as it spun, it seemed that centrifugal force might push them apart, but they stayed together, standing in a very clear and fixed relationship to each other. Julia's plaits trailed out behind her. Her eyes were wide with fright, but blank like those of a model in a store window. Willard held calmly onto his hat, his eyes staring unseeingly ahead. Coomber's eyes looked as if they were under pressure and about to pop out of his reddened face.

Phillip heard a squawking cackle. The sacred white ibis bird appeared at the centre of the tableau, like the shining hub of a wheel. It stood on a cloud, balanced on one long black leg.

'Where's Dogstar?' Phillip yelled.

'You're going to have to find him. He's gone to the other world.'

'Is that where you're taking us now – to the other side?'

The sacred ibis bird shook its head. 'Only the ferryman can take you to the other side — He Whose Face Is Turned Backwards.'

'But the ferryman isn't there any more. He gave up his ferryboat job to take tourists on boat trips along the

Nile. And his face isn't turned backwards any more. He looks forward these days.'

'You must find him.'

'Will he take us back to the same place as before?'

The bird cackled. 'Not this time. This time the journey will be even more dangerous. This time you must take an alternative route to the underworld. There are two ways to the Egyptian Fields of Offering. One is by land through the gateways of Osiris; the other — and more ancient way — is by river along the underworld Nile.

'You must journey on the infernal river like the barque of the sun, passing through the twelve deadly hours of night. At the gateways of the river you will meet the goddess of the hour who will set hideous challenges for each of you to face before your boat will be allowed safe passage to the next gateway. Fail a single challenge and your boat will be marooned in the underworld night for all eternity.'

'But I don't understand,' Phillip said. 'I left the magic scroll in a cave in the West. Surely that's where I should go to recover it.'

'It isn't there any more. It was found. It has gone to the same place as the vanished treasures of Egypt. It has been taken on the river.'

'But why?'

'Think, boy. Don't you know that in ancient Egypt everything was transported by river? It is the same in the underworld. How do you think they are carrying the heritage of Egypt back to the nether region? Do you think they are transporting pyramid blocks, stone colossi, coffins of gold and cases of treasure on their backs? By no means. They are using the river. They are carrying their prize to a guarded storehouse — the innards of the belly of the great serpent of the twelfth hour of night.'

'Will I find my dog there too?'

'Somewhere along the way, in a province of the land below.'

Phillip went giddy as blackness swarmed.

5

The ferryman

THEY HAD BROKEN OUT of the tableau and were falling to the ground. They hit, scattering like Julia's chess pieces. But it wasn't the living room floor they hit. They landed in a field of soft, cultivated, dark soil at the edge of a great stretch of river.

Phillip sat up and looked at the others. They were lying on the ground. They looked at him with the same question in their eyes.

'I've had smoother landings,' Willard Chase said, 'but we're here at last.'

'Not quite,' Phillip said. Something wasn't right. A sound in the sky above them caught his attention. He looked up at the sky and the others followed his line of vision. A passenger jet droned overhead.

'We're still in the here and now,' Julia said.

'But it's Egypt at least. I may have a rotten sense of direction, but I know the Nile,' Willard Chase said, getting up and brushing dark soil off his khaki trousers.

Julia shielded her eyes to look at the stretch of river bordered by cultivated fields.

'It's modern Egypt,' Phillip said.

'Great, we'll go sightseeing,' Coomber said sarcastically. 'Leave me out. I'm going home!'

'How do you plan to do that?' Phillip said. 'Do you think we can walk home from here? We're thousands of kilometres from home. It's just like last time. We have to stick together or none of us will ever get back.'

'What do we do now?' Julia said.

Phillip was puzzled. Why hadn't it worked? He tried to recall what had happened the last time they'd found themselves at the edge of the greatest river in history. They had found the ferryman.

The ferryman. 'We've got to look for the ferryman,' he said, remembering what the ibis bird had told him.

'You mean the ferryman who took ancient Egyptian souls to the other world, the one whose face was turned backwards?' Julia said.

'That's the one.'

'But he lived in the ancient underworld and we're in the here and now.'

'He's here too,' Phillip said. 'He was tired of living with his head turned backwards and so he turned his head around so that he could face the future. Don't you remember? He said that from now on he would take tourists on the river in his ferryboat. We must find him and ask him to turn his head back one more time — for us.'

They walked along the reed-fringed river in search of the ferryman. Lateen-masted feluccas scudded on the grey-green water. 'Look,' Julia said. She pointed to a gracious white cruise steamer, its rails jammed with tourists, heading upstream. She waved and a man on the deck fluttered his handkerchief in reply. The riverbank was like a tomb fresco come to life.

Fellahin worked in the fields, scraping at the earth with hoes and scooping water out of the river by means of a shaduf, an ancient device made of a lever and bucket. A small Egyptian girl stood under a sycamore tree. She stared at Julia shyly, twisting her skirt. A fellahin perched on a load of straw went jiggling by on a tiny, staggering donkey that looked no bigger than a dog.

'This is getting us nowhere,' Coomber said. 'Am I supposed to walk the whole length of this river?'

'I'd like to see you try,' Phillip told him, remembering the wall map in his bedroom at home. 'The Nile stretches nine thousand kilometres into the heart of Africa.'

'Great.'

'Don't give up,' Willard said. 'I see civilisation ahead.'

They reached a native village of white mud-built buildings with flat-topped roofs. The dockside was a scene of noisy activity. A stream of fellahin pressed against the travellers, carrying fruit and vegetables. A line of feluccas lay moored at the riverbank.

Barry Coomber helped himself to a bunch of grapes from a stand as they passed. Julia looked the other way in embarrassment. A trader in a bright blue *galabia* took the opportunity to offer her a live chicken, waving it by its feet in her face. She recoiled.

'Chicken!' Coomber said to her gleefully.

Beyond the marketplace they found a landing stage where a small, white, open motorboat bobbed under its gangplank. Tourists were clambering off the boat to board one of the coaches that stood by, its engine wheezing and its bodywork rattling. Another line of tourists had formed at the landing stage to go on board.

A hand-daubed sign in several languages offered a 'Scenic River Tour alongside Karnak'.

A dark man wearing sunglasses and a loose white *galabia* like a fluttering tent stood in the boat, seeing off passengers.

'We'll take the tour,' Phillip said to Willard Chase. 'Do you have any money?'

'You want to go sightseeing?' Willard Chase said.

'You don't understand. That's *him*,' Phillip whispered. 'Our ferryman from the underworld.'

'Wearing modern sunglasses?' Julia said.

'He's a forward-looking tour operator now, remember.'

'That guy always had his head screwed on the wrong way,' Coomber said. 'He gave me the creeps. You can go with him; I'll stay.'

'If you get parted from us you may never get back,' Phillip said. 'Ever. Although personally I think we'd be lucky to be rid of you so early.'

Coomber reluctantly joined the queue with the others. Willard Chase produced some US dollars from his wallet. If the ferryman recognised the group, he gave no sign of it behind the impenetrably black sunglasses. He flashed a smile of welcome as he accepted Willard's money.

Coomber gave him a suspicious scowl. Julia avoided his eye. The last time they had seen him he had been a figure of dread. He had looked very different, a bare-chested monster with his head twisted grotesquely around so that he looked permanently over his shoulder.

They chose a bench seat near the side so that they would have a better view of Karnak. The boat bobbed in the water as brightly-dressed tourists armed with cameras came on board.

The engine stuttered into life, then deepened into a low burble. They pulled away from the landing stage.

The Nile.

Once he had loved the very name. Phillip could almost forget about their mission as he released himself to the sensations of travelling on the river of mystery. It was the bloodstream of history. Its fertile banks had nourished civilisation. Phillip thought of other eyes that must have looked out on this very same stretch of water. Thutmosis. Rameses. Tutankhamen.

Yet a small, protesting voice inside him tried to rob him of his enjoyment. Once he had loved this river and its history too deeply and he had learnt a bitter lesson. He must fight his awe. It was wrong to live in the past.

More buildings appeared at the edges of the river — modern buildings, more traffic, cars and buses. They were gliding past a city. Suddenly, rearing out of the city like a giant breaking free from its chains, soared the ruins of a mighty temple. As they looked, a great column toppled over soundlessly.

'Oh no,' Willard Chase said.

Phillip looked around the boat. Nobody in their group seemed to have noticed, except the ferryman who stood at the stern, his face turned across the water, his hand frozen at the tiller.

It was the ferryman. Phillip knew it.

Their boat travelled on to another temple, divided from the river by a modern road. Great, lotus-shaped stone columns wobbled then crashed, dropping silently and slowly. Without warning, the ferryman cut the tour short. He swung his boat about and set its nose back to the landing stage.

Puzzled by his unexplained behaviour, the passengers in the boat began first to mutter then to raise their voices in protest. The ferryman went resolutely on. When he reached the landing stage, he handed back their money as they went down the gangplank. Phillip's group stayed on board.

'You must disembark,' the ferryman said, holding out the dollars that Willard Chase had given him. 'I return your money.'

'You keep it,' Phillip said, being generous with Willard's money. 'We want you to take us on a journey. We want you to take us back.'

'We cannot go back. I cannot show you the temples today.'

'We don't want to go to the temples; we want to go to the other side.'

'To the Valley of the Kings?' He shook his head. 'Even worse. I cannot show the tombs today.'

'We don't want to go to the Valley of the Kings. We want to go to the other side.'

'My boat is not for hire.'

'Not this boat. Your ferryboat. Don't you know who we are? Surely you remember us!'

'I don't know you.'

'Cast your mind back.'

'I don't look back any more.'

'Well, I know you. You are Herhaf, the ferryman, the one whose face is turned backwards. Or was.'

At the mention of his name, the ferryman pulled off the sunglasses. The eyes behind the glasses were those of an ancient Egyptian, painted like the outlines of fish with fantails at the sides. Surprise in the dark pupils of his eyes swirled like cloud nebula.

'I know your name, Herhaf, and by knowing your name I have power over you,' Phillip said. Ancient Egyptians believed that if you knew the names of the creatures in the land of the dead, you had power over them, so Phillip tried pressing the knowledge to his advantage.

'And you,' the ferryman said, 'are the boy whose face is turned backwards.'

'Not now. I don't live in the past any more; I live in the present, but I must go back one more time. We want you to take us there.'

'You want me to turn my head around again? I only look forward now,' the ferryman said.

'Then try to look forward to going back,' Phillip said.

Julia gave Phillip a warning nudge. 'Phillip, don't play word games with him,' she said in a pleading whisper. 'You'll only anger him. Don't you want him to help us? We'll never get home again!'

'Don't worry, Julia,' Phillip said in a low voice. 'The ancient Egyptians loved playing with words, especially Herhaf. It's the only way to get through to him.'

The ferryman frowned. 'You must not whisper in front of me.'

'Would you rather we whispered behind your back?'

'You are a forward boy,' the ferryman said.

'I'm sorry.'

'Well, don't whisper again. It's an affront.'

'Then let me be forthright with you. Egypt is disappearing. You can see it. It's staring you in the face. We've got to go back to stop what's happening.'

'I can't go back. I am a progressive businessman

now. I can't turn my back on my tourist operation. There are tourists to take on the river.'

'Think ahead.'

'That's all I do.'

'I don't think you're making much headway, Phillip,' Willard said, entering into the spirit of the conversation.

Coomber groaned. 'I can't face much more of this.'

Phillip ignored him. 'Look a bit further ahead, Herhaf. If there are no ancient monuments left to see, there will be no tourists coming to see them. You must agree to help us. The choice lies straight ahead.'

'It is a hard choice to make.'

'It's perfectly straightforward. Help us save Egypt or you'll be out of business. Face the fact.'

'You are turning my head with your talk, but you are right, Boy Whose Face Was Turned Backwards, even though it is a hard truth to face. I have seen what is happening. Egypt's past has been vanishing in front of my eyes.'

'Then you will help us?'

'What do you want of me? Place the facts squarely before me.'

'We need to find the underworld river. We must voyage like the sunboat through the twelve hours of night. In the belly of the great serpent, we will find a missing scroll and the lost treasures of Egypt. More importantly, we will find my dog who has disappeared. I want Dogstar back.'

'The pointy-faced one?'

'Yes. You do remember.'

'You are making my head spin, boy. Do you want me to take you on the underworld Nile? Do you know the dangers you would face in the underworld night? It is the realm of the great serpent. Read your pyramid texts and *The Book of Am Duat*.'

'What is the *Am Duat*?' Julia said.

Willard Chase explained. 'The *Am Duat* describes another path by which royalty journeyed into eternity. It is found described in the pyramid texts. When the king died it was believed that he entered the sunboat of the sky, his Boat of Millions of Years, and by this means journeyed to heaven.

'The most terrifying part of the journey was natural- ly when the sun sank for it meant that he must journey through the invisible part of the world which was called the *Am Duat*. During the twelve deadly hours of the night he was beset by terrible dangers and challenged by the eternal enemy of the sun, the great serpent, who tried to swallow the boat and so stop the sun from rising.'

'Perfect,' Coomber said bitterly.

'*The Book of Am Duat* says that there are twelve provinces of the night guarded by monsters and demons who are under the direction of the goddess of the hour. She alone can open the gate leading into the next hour. She will only do this if a password or the answer to a test is given.'

'Not exams again! I thought I'd got away from all that. The only good thing about being here is missing school,' said Coomber.

'What has brought this tragedy on Egypt?' Herhaf said.

Phillip explained to him about the scroll. 'Every- thing from Egypt is going to disappear. You're from Egypt's past,' Phillip said to the ferryman. 'If you don't help us to stop what's happening, you could be the next to fade away.'

'These are confronting arguments you advance.'

'Then you'll help us?'

'I believe you have turned me around. Yes, I must face the truth,' Herhaf said. 'Let us proceed.'

'How will we locate the underground river?' Willard said to the ferryman, uncertain, as always, about directions. 'Do you know the way?'

'This is a magical journey and to make it we must travel in a magical boat, not my old ferryboat which has now been converted into a felucca. We must find a royal barque, a sunboat of a pharaoh.'

'What's a sunboat?' Julia said.

'A sunboat was a funerary boat built to carry the dead pharaoh on his voyage through eternity,' Willard said. 'Unfortunately, there aren't too many of those lying around.'

'Weren't the remains of two sunboats found buried in boat pits near the Great Pyramid at Giza?' Phillip said.

'That's right,' Willard said. 'The first one and the best was discovered in 1954 in a hidden chamber. It was found in kit form, like a giant puzzle, with over a thousand components waiting to be pieced together. One hundred and forty-two feet long, it's the oldest ship in the world — 4 600 years old to be exact. It's now housed in a special museum alongside the pyramid.'

'Then we can't use it, ' Phillip said disappointedly.

'I'm afraid not. Besides, the boat is hardly in river-worthy condition, even though the cedar planks were remarkably well preserved and still held the fragrance of the timbers of Lebanon.'

'What are we going to do?'

'There is one more boat, undiscovered and intact,' Herhaf said. 'The only way to reach it is through a secret passage in the Great Pyramid. We must go to Giza.'

'Will you take us there in your motor boat?'

'My boat will take too long.'

'Then we'll go from Luxor on the overnight train,' Willard said.

'As long as you are paying,' the ferryman said shrewdly.

6

Pyramid boat

TO FIND THE SECRET ENTRANCE to the pyramid they should use the cover of darkness, the ferryman said; and so it was that on a star-pricked night, Herhaf and the tomb travellers crossed a stretch of desert sand on the Giza plateau to approach the deeper shadow of the Great Pyramid.

Phillip had read that the modern city of Cairo now pressed to the edges of the pyramid and that roads with buses disgorged sightseers night and day, but there was nobody to be seen on this night and no sight of city buildings except distant lights.

The darkness had a textured feeling as if dusted by the stars, Phillip thought. He lifted his head to look up at the pyramid, lit by an ailing moon that stood directly over its apex. The side of the pyramid looked like a wedge of shadow fallen from the moon as if the moon threw no light but darkness that night.

A long, tremulous animal's howl pierced the silence.

'What's that horrible noise?' Julia said, moving closer to Phillip's side.

'Just a stray dog from a village,' Phillip said, not

wanting to frighten Julia.

'No, it is the pointy-faced one,' Herhaf said. 'Anubis, the jackal god of the dead.'

'Not that character again,' Barry Coomber said edgily.

'What am I doing here again?' Julia said. 'I don't think I like being a friend of yours, Phillip. You keep dragging me along on your ghastly journeys.'

'At least you're his friend,' Coomber said. 'I hate him and still he drags me along.'

The Great Pyramid's size was impressive enough to the eye, but even more to the spirit, Phillip thought. It rose, crushing the senses, a mass of stones so vast and impassable that it seemed to tempt calamity. It not only filled his eyes, but his mind, like some unbearable situation in his life that he couldn't see past. Like the disappearance of Dogstar, he thought. 'Where are you, boy? I'm coming; just hang on.'

Here it was — the Great Pyramid, the subject of the framed picture poster that had hung in his bedroom, the poster that had fallen off the wall and shattered.

The square of the hypotenuse of a right angle triangle is equal to the sum of the squares of the other two sides. An isosceles triangle has two equal sides. An equilateral triangle has all its sides equal. Remembered bits of geometry jingled like musical triangles in Phillip's mind.

The rules of geometry did not prepare you for the reality of the pyramid, no more than studying the structure of an atom on the blackboard prepared you for a nuclear explosion. It was the most monumental protest man had ever made against death and the closest thing to eternity he had ever achieved.

A stone structure one hundred and twenty-six metres high. Made up of a million tonnes of stone, each stone weighing an average of one tonne. Enough stone to build a wall three metres high around France, Napoleon had said.

'It's quite big,' Coomber said grudgingly.

'Heard of the Empire State Building in New York?' Willard Chase said. 'That's quite big, too. I know; I've been to the top. It's so big that when I looked over the edge, the drop to the street below seemed to suck my eyes out of my head, but it's nothing compared to the Great Pyramid. If you could weigh this building in a giant balance, you could place twenty Empire State Buildings in one pan and the Great Pyramid in the other without tipping the pan.'

They were at the base of the pyramid. Herhaf stopped them and looked up.

'Do you know where the secret entrance is?' Phillip said.

'No.'

'Then how do you hope to find it?'

'It may be quite straightforward. Stand aside, a block is falling,' Herhaf said calmly.

A giant shadow of stone detached itself from the larger shadow of the pyramid's side and fell like a rockslide down a mountain. Julia screamed. They dived to one side, Julia hanging onto Phillip's arm. The whole plateau shook. It went quiet.

'Do you feel it? The ground's still trembling.'

'That's me,' Julia said.

They got up, brushing sand off themselves.

'I'm not waiting around for the next one. The whole thing's going to fall down on us,' Coomber said.

'Then we'll have to be quick,' Willard Chase said.

The ferryman looked up. 'Our answer lies before us.'

They followed Herhaf's line of vision. A shaft of rainbow-coloured light, as though refracted through a glass prism, beamed out of the pyramid from the spot where the fallen stone had stood.

'Where's that light coming from?'

'From the sunboat. We must climb,' Herhaf said. He went ahead of them, scaling the pyramid.

It wasn't exactly a stairway to heaven, Phillip thought. The stone blocks were shoulder high and they had to hoist themselves up. They toiled to the glowing entrance. Another rumble shook the stone under their feet.

'I will go ahead,' Herhaf said. The rainbow light streaming from the entrance lit his face in vivid, gaudy bands, like light from a discotheque. It was so bright that he dug into a pocket in his white *galabia* and produced sunglasses which he put on. 'Press forward,' he said, going ahead along the brightly-lit corridor. They followed him into a passage cut out of the solid rock.

Enlivening the walls were carved and painted scenes depicting a dead king's journey through the under-world night to eternity. Rows of slender-limbed goddesses swayed in profile and serpents threw their rippling coils along the corridor's length.

One scene showed a gang of monster-headed men towing the king's barque through the underworld. The king's barque was a graceful craft swept up elegantly at stem and stern. The king himself, in the form of the hawk-headed god Horus, stood in a deckhouse, wearing the image of the sun-disc on his head.

The passage they followed entered a high-vaulted gallery, then the floor dropped and turned back on itself and descended further down into the core of the pyramid and then into the bed of the plateau. Still the light shone in their faces, making them shield their eyes.

Phillip tried not to think of the crushing weight of stone over their heads as another tremor shook the passage they were following. The air was fresh, dry and faintly perfumed as if incense floated up the passage to greet them. The light grew stronger.

They reached a doorway built for a giant to enter. The ferryman stopped here and waited for the others to catch up. Bright light poured through the doorway.

'The divine sunboat of Khufu,' the ferryman said in a ringing voice, like a majordomo introducing guests. He waved them through the doorway ahead of himself. The tomb travellers entered through the doorway.

It was like going into a chamber that held the morning sun.

The divine sunboat of Khufu was a painted and gilded ship fifty metres long. It was flat-bottomed with no keel, and its stem and stern sheered elegantly upwards from its hull which was gilded at the ends and painted green at the waist. It had no mast or sail, but rows of spear-tipped oars, shipped at deck level. It had a deckhouse, enclosed with latticed screens, amidships. Its gilded stem and stern posts, in the shape of tied papyrus bundles, flared at the ends and were curved inwards to face the deckhouse.

The ship shone like the sun itself.

'Why's it so bright?' Coomber complained.

'It's a solar barque,' Willard Chase said.

'It's pretty useless here. Are we supposed to drag it to the river?'

Herhaf went to the back of the chamber where a painted wooden Djed pillar stood. 'Go on board,' he told the others. 'This pillar is a lever and when I pull it, the waters will rise, the stones will lift and we will drift into the infernal realms of night.'

The ferryman's instructions were not so easy to follow. The steep, green-and-gold sides of the hull rose smooth and impossibly high above them. To their surprise, a coiled length of *halfa* grass rope sailed over the side and hit the stone floor.

'I don't like this,' Coomber muttered. 'Who threw that rope?' The tomb travellers looked at each other uneasily.

'My crew,' Herhaf said. 'You will not see them. They are shades, the souls of oarsmen who will row us on the river. There is no wind on the Nether Nile.'

Coomber backed away from the rope. 'You first,' he said to Willard. 'I'm not going up that rope with ghosts waiting at the other end.'

Willard Chase grabbed the rope. He went up the side smartly, hand over hand like a gymnast. 'Nobody at home,' he said, looking around. 'Who's next?' he called over the side.

He helped the others up, hauling on the rope to raise them to the deck.

Phillip was the last to grab the length of *halfa* grass rope. It felt dry in his hands. Willard gave a tug at the other end. The rope rasped coarsely through Phillip's hands. He tightened his grip. The rope squeaked. He hoped it would hold him. His feet left the floor and his body swung against the hull. The aroma of cedar wood filled his lungs like perfume, as if precious embalming unguents had been used to preserve these 4 600-year-old timbers.

He reached the top and clambered over the side.

They stood on the deck in an uneasy group. They were all thinking the same thing. Who had thrown down the rope? Where were the shades of the oarsmen? The rows of shipped oars lay unattended on either side of the royal barque. Julia cast an uneasy glance at the covered deckhouse. 'I wonder what's lurking in there?'

'I'm not about to find out,' Coomber said. 'Where's the ferryman?'

They looked over the side.

Herhaf put the weight of his body against the Djed column. As he did so they heard a grating sound, followed by a rumble as if the sluice gates of a dam had been opened. Dark water burst into the chamber.

Herhaf ran to the waiting rope and climbed. Phillip and Willard grabbed the other end and pulled hard to speed his climb. Even so the water swirled around his legs, twisting his body on the rope. The sunboat stirred and came alive with creaking sounds and the groans of ancient timbers waking after a sleep of millennia. Phillip hoped it would still float. What if the timbers had warped?

They dragged Herhaf over the side. Dark water now boiled around the pyramid boat, but still there was nowhere to go. A solid stone wall faced the prow. Was it some kind of water lock? Herhaf went with a purposeful air to the stern where he took hold of a mighty rudder, a single steering oar that passed through the hull. Unexpectedly, he stood with his back to the prow. He was facing the wrong way. Were they going to travel backwards?

The ferryman corrected his ideas. 'Before I go back to the netherworld, I must turn my head around,' he said. Then he gave a pained cry and, once again with a crack like a breaking spar, he turned his head around to face backwards.

'Welcome back, Herhaf,' Phillip said.

The sunboat rose and lifted off the floor. Willard Chase checked the level of the rising water over the side, then looked up at the stone roof above them. 'If something doesn't happen soon, we're going to drown in here like rats.'

Herhaf did not look perturbed. The impossibly twisted face behind the sunglasses remained impassive. Herhaf knew what to expect. When the sunboat looked in danger of reaching the stone ceiling, the blocks of stone in the front of the chamber fell away like a creature dropping its lower jaw and they swept out of the chamber and onto a river of impenetrable night, riding on a current.

Their eyes, at first blinded, grew accustomed to the dark. The barque itself glowed, lighting the deck and throwing light some distance to a riverbank where darkness ruled, but even here the darkness was not total. The bank was lit with tiny lights like an aircraft runway.

'What are those lights, Ferryman?' Phillip asked.

'They are serpents who spit flames,' Herhaf said. 'We have entered the first vestibule.'

'Snakes?' Julia said, shuddering. 'I hope they don't swim.'

They were drifting, but at a command from the ferryman in a language Phillip did not understand, the spear-shaped oars rumbled out on both sides of the pyramid boat and hit the water with a splash. The oars, still unattended, began to sway. Stems creaked and blades splashed as unseen backs bent to the work. Phillip felt his spine tingle. The boat gathered speed. They heard sighs of effort from the shadow oarsmen.

'I don't like this,' Coomber said.

'Don't complain,' Julia said. 'At least we're getting away from the snakes.'

'It is not the snakes you have to fear,' the ferryman said. 'It is the first gateway which bars our way ahead. There the goddess of the hour will appear and set the first challenge.'

7

Gateway of the first hour

IT SEEMED AT FIRST SIGHT to be a dam wall — like the High Dam at Aswan — with some kind of beacon perched on top, but as the sun barque drew nearer, Phillip saw that it was a fortress spanning the river. It had crenellations and buttresses and towers and a gateway with massive pylons on either side. The beacon was no beacon either, Phillip saw, changing his opinion. It was moving. They made out the glowing figure of a woman walking across the top of the wall.

'The goddess of the hour,' the ferryman said.

The woman's body was dotted with pinpoints of light like faraway stars.

'She's beautiful!' Julia whispered in admiration. 'Who is she?'

'The ancient Egyptian sky goddess,' Willard said. 'Her name is Nut. She personifies the vault of heaven. The ancient Egyptians believed that the stars of night travelled through her body which was arched across the earth, her feet touching the eastern horizon and her hands the west.

'She was the mother of the sun and some believed that each sunset she swallowed the sun-disc which travelled through her body to be born again each morning. She has power over all the demons and guardians here, so don't try to trick her. Or the sky will fall in.'

'Prepare for the first test,' the ferryman said.

'Exams again,' Barry Coomber grumbled.

The ferryman steered the pyramid boat between the two pylons. They entered a lock. The unseen oarsmen shipped oars and they berthed at a stone quay. Unseen hands magically ran out a gangplank. The goddess of the hour came down from the wall to wait for them at the quay.

'Look at her. Her body is made up entirely of stars,' Julia said. 'Thousands of them.'

Her features were typically ancient Egyptian — small-chinned, shrewdly beautiful. The dark-as-tomb eyes were lined with make-up that widened into deltas of purple at the sides and the eyelids were dusted with fine stars. 'You must disembark,' Herhaf said, 'and do as the lady of the hour tells you or you shall never enter the first section of the night and never go back.'

'She doesn't frighten me. I'm not going to be pushed around by a lady in fancy dress with spangles stuck all over her body,' Coomber said.

Emboldened by his own boast, Barry Coomber led the way down the gangplank onto the quay. He went directly to the glowing figure, his hands in his pockets, and he confronted her with a glare. 'We want to go back home, Lady, so please open your gate. We're out of school now and we don't want to go through a bunch of boring tests — if it's all the same to you.'

Phillip stiffened. How would she react to Coomber's brazen challenge? Would the sky fall in? The sky swallowed them instead.

The pinpoints of light that held the woman's body together began to spin and separate. Her body stretched and stretched then, with a whoosh and a shower of stars like a skyrocket going off, she arched over their heads from one horizon to the other.

Phillip lost sight of the others. He found himself under a spinning vault of stars, terribly and frighteningly alone. It was freezing here and the stars in the sky looked cold and faint.

Two larger stars appeared, staring unblinkingly down at him. Was she watching him? He felt her alien, pagan stare. What was he expected to do — beg for mercy?

He called out the names of the others, but the endless space sucked his cries away into emptiness. He had never felt so alone in his life. There was not just an absence of people; there was a vacuum created by their going that tugged at his feelings. They had all vanished. Dogstar, now Julia, Willard and Barry Coomber.

He gave a cry of loneliness.

'Don't be afraid; you are never alone,' something told him, but that something was not the star-lady above, but another, the one he had met on his last journey, the one who would never leave him.

'I'm not alone,' he said to the stars. 'Even here. There's nowhere that you or even my imagination can take me where I'll be totally alone, so take me back and we'll face your test.'

He saw a shooting star, then another. The stars,

widely spaced in the heavens, drew together. The vault around him closed like a desert flower at night. In a blink he found himself back with the others, standing at the quay in front of the lady of the hour.

'Those fireworks were huge!' Coomber said. 'But I didn't like it when the lights went out. It reminded me of when I was a little kid and my mum shut me in the cupboard under the stairs.'

'Shut up, Barry Coomber,' Julia said. 'Do you want to get us into more trouble?'

'Who will face the first test?' the lady of the hour said in a tubular-sounding voice that sounded as if it had rolled around the stars before it reached their ears. 'The first test is a trial by magic.'

Julia looked at Barry Coomber. 'You're pretty good at making things disappear,' she told him acidly. 'You go first.'

'What sort of magic?' Coomber said to the star woman in a slightly more respectful tone than before. 'You mean magic tricks?'

'A contest of magic — and a mystery.'

'No thanks. You go, Willard; you're the archaeological detective.'

The lady of the hour took the decision out of their hands. 'You have chosen yourself. You will face the test, vile boy,' she told Barry Coomber. 'Follow.'

The lady went ahead of them, disappearing into a hallway.

'Thanks for dropping me in it, Julia.'

'You did it yourself.'

Barry Coomber went after the lady and the others followed. They found themselves in a hall. A brightly-lit stage occupied its centre. On the stage stood frozen characters waiting for a cue to begin a performance. It was like a scene from a tomb painting. At the centre of it lay the figure of a pharaoh on a couch, attended by his courtiers.

The lady of the hour set the scene like the chorus in a Greek drama:

Here is the mystery of the Rameses harem conspiracy. Listen closely because your life depends on your answer to it. One of the king's favourite wives is conspiring to kill the king by means of a magic scroll which she has obtained. It is a book of witchcraft and she is using it to practise powerful magic against the king's life.
The king has called his court magicians to try to find the guilty wife. You are one of the court magicians. You must defeat the other two rival magicians in a trial by magic. You must prove who is the guilty wife and save the king's life, but you may use only the tools of magic that the other two court magicians use. How will you do it? And remember, you may only act here and are forbidden to enter the harem which is barred to all but the king and his wives.

Phillip and the others squatted on the floor like an audience attending a play. Barry Coomber went closer, standing at the edge of the pool of light.

'You will enter the scene and join the court magicians,' the sky goddess said, standing in the shadows, the stars in her body glowing like moths around a lamp.

Barry Coomber joined the two magicians and looked around at the assembled characters. They paid no attention to him as if they were expecting his arrival.

Phillip's eyes went to the king who was attended by a personal physician, a vizier and two court magicians.

Was this shrivelled man who lay, or rather shrank, among cushions on a leopard-headed couch, the Pharaoh Rameses who had turned back the invading fleet of the Sea Peoples?

Phillip turned his attention to the magicians. One was a small fat man with a neck like a bull, the other a towering black Nubian.

The vizier, who was the king's chief minister, approached the royal magicians, including Barry Coomber, and paced the floor thoughtfully in front of them, like an ibis wading in the shallows of the Nile. He was composing a speech, it turned out.

'The harem is a flower,' the vizier said in a reedy, cultivated voice, 'a beautiful scented flower that delights the heart of His Majesty. And like a flower, the harem is guarded by thorns, a royal bodyguard armed with spears, but inside the walls of scented petals there is the buzz of intrigue — and death lies waiting to give its sting.'

After this flowery speech, the vizier swung on each of the practitioners in turn, looking for their reaction. He found none in the face of the black Nubian sorcerer; it was a face fashioned in planes of dark obsidian stone. The other magician with the bull neck was more appreciative, rewarding his words with a sober nod of appreciation. Finally his eye fell on Barry Coomber. Coomber looked bored already. He yawned.

'Death lies waiting to give its sting,' the king's chief minister said more emphatically. 'A case of witchcraft in the House of the Secluded.' Coomber sneered at the mention of witchcraft. His manner angered the great man, who said directly to him: 'A plot against His Majesty.'

When Barry Coomber did not register sufficient horror, the vizier stopped in front of him. 'You take this announcement with wondrous calm, young magician.'

Coomber shook his head. 'You don't believe in a lot of rot like magic, do you? Magic is just for party tricks.'

'Do you think so?' The vizier crossed to a table. A vase stood on the table and beside it a roll of linen cloth. An object bulked inside the cloth. Phillip saw the king stir in his cushions, fingering an amulet on his wrist as the vizier picked up the bundle and unrolled it, using long fingers of distaste. He would not touch the object he revealed, but left it exposed on the cloth on the table.

'You call this a party trick?' he said to Barry Coomber.

Coomber went nearer, along with the other sorcerers. He dipped into the spread of cloth and pulled out the object which he held up and turned around in his fingers. It was an effigy. The king groaned, clutching his head. The effigy in wax was shaped in the image of the king. It sprouted more spikes from its head than a porcupine.

'What do you say now, sorcerer?' the vizier said in a voice that was like the warning hiss of a snake.

'A girl's doll,' Coomber said. 'It can't do any harm.'

At this point, the king's personal physician, who had been silent, gave a cluck of impatience. 'What about the curse incised in the wax? You don't find curses on a girl's doll.'

Barry Coomber eyed it sceptically, the other two magicians moving nearer. The small magician gasped as he read it. It must have been a curse of a particularly shuddersome nature, which he dared not read aloud in the king's presence. It brought a murmur of admiration from his colleague the Nubian.

'How do you interpret such a spell?' the physician said, coming over to join the sorcerers. Barry Coomber put the doll back onto the table beside the vase. The doctor, a big, sober-eyed man, leaned forward on widely spread feet in a way that was bullying. Even though he was a man of science, a specialist in medicine, he was obviously taking the whole thing seriously.

Watching the confrontation between the doctor and Coomber, Phillip reminded himself that physicians in Egypt were part sorcerers, part sawbones. Doctors and magicians were colleagues in sister professions. 'Just words,' Coomber said scornfully. 'Mumbo jumbo. It's not even English.'

'And you call yourself a magician?' the doctor leaned forward even more bullyingly. 'Even I can tell that it is a virulent curse directed against the king.' The king groaned, fingering imaginary spikes in his skull.

The physician went on. 'How do you explain the fire that burns in the royal head?'

The vizier, who felt he was losing the floor, cleared his throat. 'Virulent indeed — a spell from a most authoritative source. In fact, we know the source.' He paused for effect. 'Recently,' the vizier continued in his reedy voice, 'a secret magical scroll went missing from the royal library – someone stole it in order to practise black art. Fortunately, it was found in a chamber beneath the harem walls.'

The king's groan was loud enough to cut the vizier short. 'Take these red hot spears from my skull, physician!' the king said.

The physician went to the king. From a box he took out a pen and ink and a roll of papyrus. He was scribbling a prescription, Phillip guessed. He wondered which powerful drug the doctor had selected from Egypt's vast pharmacopoeia.

To his surprise, the physician tore off a strip of papyrus and held it up, saying, 'It is sorcery that afflicts His Majesty. And it is sorcery alone that can alleviate the pain. A magical headache formula,' he told the three sorcerers, a reminder that he, too, was a subject of Thoth, god of sorcery and learning, as well as owing allegiance to Imhotep, god of medicine.

Next the physician called for a jug of water and, placing the scrap into a cup, he filled the cup with liquid. Barry Coomber looked instantly suspicious. The risk was clear. What if there were poison in the papyrus or in the ink?

'Stop right there. You say you're a doctor, but you're acting like a magician. Maybe you're one of the magicians in the puzzle. Are you trying to poison the king?' The physician raised an eyebrow. Had Barry Coomber solved the mystery already?

The physician smiled. Baitingly, he said to Coomber, 'Perhaps you will taste it for the king.'

'No thanks. You made it, you taste it.'

All eyes turned on the physician. Would he drink it? He did. The physician raised the cup and sipped. Phillip wondered what he could taste. The sharp clench of swiftly acting poison, or simply the sooty taste of carbon and the faint tang of resin, the chief constituents of Egyptian ink?

'I am still alive, see?' The physician now gave the cup to the king who slurped the rest of it eagerly down, afterwards giving a long, shivery sigh. He looked around at the sorcerers, blinking at them as if aware of his surroundings for the first time. The doctor bowed. The small fat-necked magician beside Coomber murmured in approval.

'Thankyou, physician,' the vizier said, returning his attention to the three sorcerers. 'You have now heard the circumstances of this alarming matter. Do your work to protect the king.'

He clapped his hands. 'Here are the royal wives, the six favourites, the only ones who have had access to the king and the harem where the doll was found.' A row of heavily painted ladies in gauzy white dresses and with beehive wigs on their heads filed into the chamber and stood in a row.

Barry Coomber spoke to the vizier. 'Is it okay if I ask them some questions?'

'No.'

'How am I supposed to discover the culprit without talking to them? Do you think I'm a magician?'

'Precisely. Use your magic.'

'One more question. How long have I got?'

'Time has no reality here. Take as long as you like, but to pass the test you must be the first magician to solve the mystery.' As if to make it even more clear, the vizier added: 'You must be the one who saves the king from the attacks of evil forces by means of your powers. Now which one of you gentlemen will try his powers first?'

The small, squat sorcerer stepped forward. 'I will quickly counteract any evil influence here,' he said in a ringing bull-like voice. He picked up a vase from the table where it stood beside the effigy and raised the vase high above his head and spoke words of power: 'All men, all people, all folk, all males, all eunuchs, all females, all concubines and all nobles, who may rebel, who may plot, who may fight, who may think of fighting or who may think of rebelling against the king, and every rebel who thinks of rebelling – in the entire land.'

The vizier widened his eyes.

The magician built his voice into a towering obelisk: 'Every evil word, every evil speech, every evil slander, every evil thought, every evil plot, every evil fight, every evil quarrel, every evil plan, every evil thing, every evil dream, and all evil — I hereby *s-m-a-s-h!*' With this, the sorcerer hurled the vase to the painted floor where it broke with a most satisfying bang that drained the colour from the vizier's face.

'That vase — was priceless,' the vizier said forlornly, looking at the scattered pieces. 'It was antique Old Kingdom!'

'That, Sir, only adds to the efficacy of the curse,' the magician assured him.

Barry Coomber laughed scornfully. 'You call that a good magic trick? I'd be more impressed if you could stick all the bits together again and fix the vase. Go ahead, I dare you!'

'Sir!' the magician said, hurt. 'You mock me.'

'Well, that was pathetic. You can't spout a lot of dumb words and expect it to achieve something.'

'I fear the young magician may be right,' the vizier said, looking sceptically at the small magician. He turned to the towering black magician. 'And what is your protection, Nubian?' Then he added quickly: 'But no more destruction of royal property, please.'

The Nubian opened a box that carried the tools of his trade, taking out a mound of yellow wax.

'Ah, magic wax,' the vizier said, relieved. 'That's tidier.'

With nimble fingers, the Nubian broke it into six pieces and from these pieces fashioned six human forms, pinching in each at the waist to lend them vaguely feminine proportions. These six dumpy ladies he stood in a row on the floor under his melting gaze. Everyone watched, even the king lifting himself up on one elbow, for there was an intensity in the Nubian's attention to his work that compelled interest.

He now took two burning torches from stands in the chamber and, arms swirling, performed a convulsive dance within hoops of flame, punctuating it with hisses like those of an angry black snake.

Barry Coomber seemed impressed by the performance itself, but looked scornful about its magical implications, unlike the others in the scene, all of whom appeared captivated, except for one, Phillip noted — the physician, who stifled a yawn. The magical and medical professions were very close and held little mystery for each other.

Giving a final hiss, the Nubian fell to his knees before the wax dolls. Swiftly he brought the twin flames of the torches over the wax figures, passing them back and forth above the row so that each doll appeared to pass through a trial of fire. The model wives soon trickled hot tears of wax onto the floor — all but one.

After a few more passes, five of the six waxen wives were reduced to stubs — one alone stood intact. Again the black man ran the flames across the row of figures.

Was he sparing one doll from the flames? Barry Coomber was watching him very closely. The magician's movements were smooth and even and it was difficult to tell.

Finally, five wives lay in pools of wax. The sixth, defying the flame, stood mockingly whole amid the hardening pools.

'She!' the black man hissed. 'I will stop her!' He raised a large unsandalled foot and crushed the doll under a calloused heel. It put a brutal end to the doll and to the performance. With an air of completion, the black man stepped back and folded his arms across his chest.

Making an effort, the vizier restored his detached composure. 'Must these magicians make a mess?' he muttered to himself. He turned his attention to Barry Coomber.

'And what, young man, is your offering?'

Phillip recalled the rules that the sky goddess had set. Coomber could only choose one of the means of magic that he had seen displayed. Would he choose sympathetic magic, the breaking of a vase, would he use the wax dolls — or perhaps use a written spell in a cup as the physician had done? The physician was part magician and had to be included in any reckoning.

Coomber paced. He stopped to stare at the physician, then at the pieces of broken vase on the floor and finally at the pools of melted wax.

'Um,' he said.

'Well?' the vizier prodded him.

'I reckon the best thing now would be a good night's sleep.'

'Sleep, I confess, would be welcome, but is this all

you can offer?'

'Right now, yes. It's getting late and frankly you can't expect magic this time of night.'

The bull-necked magician whispered hoarsely behind him: 'Have a care for the reputation of our profession, young man.' He cleared his throat and spoke up on Coomber's behalf: 'My young colleague here means, of course, to use his powers of dream divination.'

'I see.'

'Not exactly,' Barry Coomber said. 'Let's say the power of sleeping on a problem.' What was Barry Coomber doing? Phillip wondered.

The vizier shrugged. 'Then you'd better get to work. It's late. Good night, gentlemen.'

'Before you go, I want to make a little gift to each of the wives.'

'What gift?'

'I don't have it. I said I want to make it.'

Now Barry Coomber went to the black magician's box and took out another lump of magic wax. He squatted on the floor and began to roll the lump into a long cylinder like a snake. 'This reminds me of playing with plasticine back in pre-school,' he said, 'only it doesn't stink like plasticine.'

'More mess,' the vizier complained, looking weary.

'Coomber's flipped out,' Julia whispered. 'It's the pressure.'

'I'm not so sure,' Willard Chase said.

Coomber broke the lengthened roll of wax into six pieces, then, just as the Nubian had done, he fashioned each piece into a female shape, pinching it in at the waist. When he had finished his work, another row of dumpy ladies stood on the stone floor.

'There,' he said, scooping them up into the corner of his arm. 'I have six dolls for the king's wives to take to bed with them.' He got up and approached the row of king's wives. 'Goodnight ladies,' he said, handing a doll to the first of them. The lady looked reluctant to touch it, but at a nod from the vizier she took it from Coomber's hand.

He went on down the line, handing a wax doll to each wife. 'You can keep these dolls overnight, but bring them back with you tomorrow morning. Just a warning, though. These dolls are made of magic wax and, after the heat of the night, one of the dolls will tell me which one of you is the guilty one. Watch them carefully.'

The vizier clapped his hands and the wives filed out of the chamber. Coomber came back to the vizier, wiping his wax-covered hands as if he were finished with the matter. 'Now let's get some shut-eye.'

'Go and wait in the shadows,' the vizier said. He pointed to where the other tomb travellers sat. 'And await the dawn.'

The pool of light in the chamber went out as if a curtain had come down on a scene and a few minutes later, like a play, the light came on again and the wives filed back into the chamber and stood in a row.

'That's what I call a cat-nap,' Willard quipped.

Barry Coomber looked eager to resume. 'Now for the fun part,' he said. He went to the row of royal wives. 'Show me your dolls.'

They held them up and Barry Coomber walked down the row, stopping to look at each.

He never reached the last wife.

He stopped at the fifth wife and pointed at her. 'This is the guilty wife.'

She took a faltering step back. 'Give me your doll,' Coomber demanded. She hid the doll against her chest. 'Give it!' the vizier commanded her.

She held it out with a reluctant hand.

Coomber took it, smiled at it and held it up for the others to see.

The wax doll was melted down to a mere stump.

'All the royal wives have brought back their dolls and all the dolls are unchanged, except one, this one, the one that belongs to the guilty wife. Look at it. She's turned a blowtorch on it!'

Coomber gave her an accusing look and she flashed resentment at him. 'Let me explain,' he said, enjoying himself. 'The guilty wife was obviously hooked on magic or she'd never have practised magic against the king in the first place. She planted the magical doll with spikes in its head because she believed in the power of magic.

'Being a believer in magic, she would also have been convinced by the Nubian's magical performance. She saw what happened when the Nubian magician ran his flames over the wax dolls. The innocent ones all melted. The guilty one, magically, survived the flames.

'When I gave her the doll made of magic wax to keep overnight, she was afraid. She knew that she was guilty and believed that her doll would give her away. She thought the other wives' dolls would melt in the heat of the night, but not hers and so point the finger of guilt at her.

'I reckon she probably stared at it all night, willing it to melt. When it didn't and threatened to give her away, she held it over a lamp to melt. Hers is the only doll melted. She melted it herself. Her own faith in dumb magic has caught her out.'

The guilty wife gave a cry. An invisible flame turned a blast of heat on her body. She melted like a wax doll, running hot, waxen tears over the cold stone floor. The vizier bowed to Barry Coomber.

Barry Coomber grinned smugly over his shoulder at the others in the dark. 'Beat that,' he said. 'I've had my turn. Now I can sit back and watch the rest of you sweat.'

Willard Chase did not hide his admiration. 'Brilliant solution.'

'I thought so,' Coomber said.

'He's going to be impossible after this,' Julia said.

'Good work, Coomber,' Phillip said.

'Yeah, well let's see you do as well,' Coomber said gloatingly.

Barry Coomber made it hard for others to admire him, Phillip thought, but he did admire him a bit after solving the Rameses harem mystery.

The scene and the characters disappeared. They were alone with the goddess of the hour.

'Well played, vile boy. You are all free to pass into the first hour of night. The second test will occur not at the second gate, but on the river itself.'

'What is the next test?' Julia said.

'You must hold off the hordes of seekers of light for one hour. For a weapon you will have only words. You must tell the seekers of light a tale that will enthral them for an hour. Or you will perish.'

8

The seekers of light

THEY PASSED THROUGH THE GATEWAY into the first hour of the underworld night. 'Who are the seekers of light?' Julia asked.

The ferryman — the one whose face is turned backwards — who stood at the stern, manning the long steering oar, answered: 'Casting my mind back, I recall that the first division of the *Am Duat* is filled with the souls of the departed who are not able to pass any further. They throng here in their millions. Listen and you will hear their moans.'

Phillip listened. Yes, he heard them — moaning sounds, like the sough of wind through a forest — sounds of sadness, but also of reverence and awe.

'They are adoring the light we shed. To them, magically, our boat is the sun itself. We are bringing them life with our light. The air that we carry with us lets them breathe again, but only for one hour. We must hold them off for an hour or join them for eternity.'

'How awful,' Julia said, peering at the riverbank. 'Where are they? I can't see them.'

'You will see them soon enough. And you will see them for all eternity if you fail in the test that is coming,' the ferryman said.

'There they come,' Phillip said. Forms were moving in the gloom — millions of human forms, densely swarming like ants in an ants' nest.

The river grew shallow. The forms waded out to their sunboat, their arms upraised in adoration. The sound of their moans grew like massed choirs of sorrow.

'If you do not succeed in holding them off,' Herhaf said, 'they will swamp us and turn our boat over.'

'Let's grab some oars and clobber them,' Coomber suggested.

'That will not help. They number more than grains of sand in the desert. You must use words as your defence.'

'That's what the lady of the hour said,' Julia recalled. 'Somebody must tell a tale to hold off the seekers of light for an hour.'

'Who knows a tale that will shed light in their lives?' the ferryman asked.

'Yeah, who knows any good stories?' Coomber said. 'I know a few jokes, but they don't go for an hour. Besides, I've had my turn. One of you can sweat it out next.'

'I don't think a joke will quite do it,' Willard Chase said. 'In fact this whole situation's far from a joke.'

'Whoever heard of a story stopping anything?' Phillip said.

'It's happened before. Don't you know about Scheherezade and the One Thousand and One Nights?' Willard said. 'Scheherezade was the new wife of a capricious Persian monarch. Disappointed with the infidelity of his wives, the shah developed the habit of taking a new wife each night and putting her to death next morning. The clever Scheherezade saved herself from the executioner's blade by her wits and her inventiveness. She captivated the shah by spinning tales night after night, tales that the monarch couldn't bear to bring to an end. She kept him amused and saved her neck for one thousand and one nights.'

'I suppose we're lucky,' Julia said. 'We only have to hold them off for an hour.'

'But what will we tell them?'

'Decide among you who will tell the tale,' the ferryman said. 'The seekers of light are drawing close.'

The unseen rowers slowed, then stopped rowing. They shipped oars. The sun barque was no longer under way. The seekers of light had grabbed hold of the hull. Their heads broke the surface of the river in a million places like rocky cataracts in the Nile. Their moans washed over the decks like waves. Phillip looked into the adoring faces of the departed ones in the water. The river was filled with heads and waving arms. They pushed against the hull. The boat began to rock.

'I'll tell them a story, like Sheherezade,' Julia said, volunteering.

'No, I'll tell it,' Phillip said. 'We don't want to waste your turn on a story. What if we need your skills later for a game? Do you remember the senet match you played against the great ape last time? We'd still be there if you hadn't taken your turn.'

'Then I'll go,' Willard said. 'I can spin some yarn or other.'

'Also risky,' Phillip said. 'What if we come across an archaeological mystery later and we've wasted your turn? No, I'll go.'

'Do you know a story you can share with them, Phillip?' Julia said, 'something that will enthral them for an hour?'

'Not really,' Phillip said.

'Yes you do — and it's no good knowing it unless you share it.'

'Share what?'

'The light.'

'What light?'

'Don't you know? I thought you found it on our last journey. If you have, you mustn't keep it to yourself. You must learn to share it. You can't keep it hidden.'

'I don't know what you mean.'

'Then I must tell it. I won't make up a story. I won't trick these poor souls. They are here craving the light, even the pale light of our sunboat. I won't distract them for an hour. If they want the light then I'll give them light. I'll give them real light.'

'What light? What are you talking about, Julia?'

'You know. You're not in the dark like those souls out there.' She seemed disappointed in him. 'Help me up onto the deckhouse,' she said. 'I'll go up where they can see me.'

Phillip cupped his hands like a stirrup to take Julia's foot and hoisted her up to the roof of the deckhouse. Julia straightened on the roof. She turned in a full circle to sweep the multitude who stretched into the distance, jamming the watercourse like a river of human heads. They cheered.

'You want the light?' she said in a clear, carrying voice, 'Then be quiet and listen. I'll give it to you. I'll share the light with you, the light that's inside me.' The boat stopped rocking. The moaning subsided.

'Once a baby was born and this baby was the light of the world. . .' She told the story simply to the multitudes, not in a preachy way, but in a young person's words, about the light of the world that had come down among ordinary people. And as she spoke the millions of souls fell quiet.

She told the story from its beginning, where a helpless baby lay in a crib in a stable, to its end, where a triumphant man left a tomb and overcame death. When she had finished she said to them all: 'There. I've given you more than an hour's light. I've brought you a light that will last forever.'

Then Phillip knew what he should have said and done and promised himself that he would try to remember to do it in future. The inhabitants of the first hour waded peacefully back to the shore. The tomb travellers rowed on and through the open gates into the province of the second hour of night.

9

Pharaoh hounds and jackals

IN THE SECOND HOUR they travelled through dimly seen fields. 'We are passing through the fields of the grain gods,' Herhaf told them. 'This is an hour of rest. We will not be tested here and will face no danger until the next gate bars our way.'

'You mean we can relax for a while?' Coomber said. 'Great. I'll grab a nap in the deckhouse.' He went to the entrance. Nobody had been inside the deckhouse yet. They had been too busy facing the challenges.

'Is it all right if we go in there, Herhaf?' Phillip said.

The ferryman shook his head. 'Not yet. Some of you will go in there later. It is the hidden room. Don't be in a hurry to go in there. There are mysteries in the hidden room.'

Barry Coomber stopped. 'The hidden room? What's lurking in there — a dead pharaoh or something?'

'Each person will find something different in the hidden room, according to his need. The goddess of the hour will tell you when you must go inside. In the hidden room you will meet your secret fears. You will find the past that you must face before you can come out of the dark into the dawn.'

'You mean there's something nasty in there?'

'Only what is inside you, whatever that might be. There is nothing in the room that you have not brought with you.'

'I'll rest on the deck, thanks.'

'Me too,' Julia said. Phillip and Willard joined them. They flopped down onto the smooth cedar deck, their backs resting against the bulwark. Willard pushed his hat over his face and dozed. Barry Coomber, tired after his mental exertion, curled up and went to sleep.

Phillip looked up at a sky that had no stars. The absence of them made him think of another absence and another star. Dogstar.

He could feel the dog's presence, its loneliness out there without him. He listened to the rhythmic splash of the oars, the creak of the ancient vessel's timbers. He was drawing close, very close to Dogstar on this infernal river of darkness. 'We're coming closer, 'Star boy. Can you feel it, too? I'm going to save you, just like you saved us.'

'What are you thinking about, Phillip?' Julia asked. 'Dogstar?'

Julia often read what was on his mind and knew what was bothering him — sometimes, it seemed, before he knew it himself.

'I can feel Dogstar watching me, longing for us to come.'

'We won't let him down,' Julia promised.

They dozed for a while. Phillip dreamt of Dogstar.

He dreamt that he saw the dog running in the heavens. It seemed a natural place to see the pharaoh hound.

Dogstar took his name from the Dog Star, a star known to the Greeks as Sirius. It was the most important star in the Egyptian zodiac, its rising in the heavens marking the season of inundation when the Nile rose and gave the silt of life to the land so that crops could grow. Phillip's Uncle William, the Egyptologist, had given him the dog and named it for him, hoping that one day it would guide Phillip just as the legendary star had guided the lives of the ancients.

Phillip dreamt that Dogstar shone in the heavens, running ahead of their boat to help the ferryman set his course.

'The third gateway bars our way,' the ferryman called.

The travellers woke up, rubbing their eyes. Phillip squinted up at the sky. There was no sign of Dogstar in the sky. It had been a dream.

Another long line of fortifications and giant pylons stretched palely across the river.

They looked for the goddess of the hour. She wasn't on the wall this time. They found her waiting for them at the quay.

Herhaf guided the boat to the quay and the crew of shades moored the boat, running out the gangplank.

They disembarked onto the quay. The sky lady turned and led the way between massive portals. They followed. She led them to a painted stone floor out in the open under the sky. The area was illuminated by lamps on stands.

Phillip inspected the floor. It looked like a giant board game of some sort. It was square at one end and rounded at the top and slightly indented at the waist. A painted palm tree, possibly a decorative piece, divided the board game into two halves. Running around the edges of the board and following the curves were holes set in parallel rows, each hole clearly demarcated by a painted ring. Evidently playing pieces were meant to go in the holes, but were absent.

'This trial is the game of hounds and jackals,' the goddess of the hour said. 'Who will play?'

A game? Who better to play a game than Julia? Phillip looked hopefully at Julia. Would they let her play? Julia had already taken her turn.

'I'll play,' she said confidently.

The sky goddess shook her head. 'No, child of light, you have already faced a challenge. Another must play the game.'

The sky goddess clapped her hands. Five black jackals loped out of the dark and like foxes each ran to a hole on the board where it sat with its head and sharp, pointed snout revealed. The jackals filled an inner row of holes closest to the painted palm tree.

The goddess of the hour clapped her hands again and this time five slender pharaoh hounds sped out of the dark and chose the opposite row of holes nearest the palm, also sitting in the holes, with their shoulders, heads and pricked ears showing.

Five Dogstars.

Phillip gaped. Was one of these pharaoh hounds Dogstar?

A broad-chested man with a black jackal's head now came out of the dark and stood on the opposite side of the board, behind the line of jackals.

'Anubis,' Willard whispered.

The lady of stars spoke. 'Who will play against Anubis, Lord of the Westerners, in a game of hounds and jackals?'

Phillip stepped forward at once. 'I'll play.'

'I'm sorry, Phillip,' Julia said. 'I tried. I'd gladly play in your place.'

Phillip would gladly have let her. Now the fate of the travellers — and Dogstar — rested with him. He didn't have Julia's talent, or her hunger for games, or her deadly intensity of play.

'I'm playing this game for Dogstar as well as for us,' Phillip said with determination. 'I'll try my very hardest.'

'Do you know the rules of contest?' the goddess of the hour said.

'No.'

The goddess of the hour explained the rules of the game. The game was controlled by throws of three knucklebone dice. The purpose of the game was to move around the board and try to take up positions in the opponent's home base. If you landed on a hole already occupied, the dog or the jackal in the hole would be attacked and would perish. Any of the animals could be moved, depending on the scores achieved with the dice.

'It's something like backgammon,' Julia said, swiftly grasping the principle of the game.

'That's fine, Julia, except I don't play backgammon.'

'It's easy. Just don't be too eager. Don't go out too fast. Keep some of your hounds in their home base to block your opponent from trying to invade. And don't be distracted. They've chosen Dogstar look-alikes in order to throw you. Very clever of them.'

'No assistance!' the lady of the hour rapped out like a school teacher. 'Go into the shadows and wait.' Julia, Willard and Coomber drew back to watch.

Phillip surveyed his row of hounds in their foxholes. Was Dogstar among them? There was no way of telling. They had their backs to him. If one of these hounds was Dogstar then it was under some kind of spell. It had shown no flicker of recognition at the sight of its master.

Which hound should he avoid moving? He could be putting Dogstar in danger. Imagine if he sacrificed Dogstar without knowing! He tensed.

'Throw the dice to see who begins.'

The jackal-headed man came forward first and picked up three large bones. They must have been the knucklebones of a giant. Each was the size of a child's fist. He tossed the dice in the air and they fell to the painted stone floor with a clatter.

'Five,' the goddess said.

Phillip now picked up the bones. They were lighter than they looked. He threw them into the air and they tumbled onto each other and scattered like children's toy blocks.

'Six. The boy begins. Make your opening move,' the goddess commanded Phillip. 'You must move one of your hounds six spaces, moving along the outside row of holes. In order to make a move, you need only point at the hound that you wish to move and then point at the hole he must occupy. He will get up and move. The hounds are charmed and must obey.'

Which hound was Dogstar? He walked up and down the row. Was this one Dogstar? Or that one? It was impossible to say. He walked around them and went onto the board to look at their faces. Yes, that one had the eyes of Dogstar, but that one had the ears. So did that one. Maybe it was the next one. Or even the next. Phillip began to sweat. He felt Julia's eyes willing him to make the right move.

'Move,' the goddess said again, 'or forfeit a piece.' Phillip's hands slid nervously into his pockets and his fingers met a small loop of leather. Dogstar's collar. He had vowed to put it back on the dog's neck, but would he have the chance if he failed? He studied the nearest pharaoh hound.

Thinking of the collar in his pocket, his eye went to the animal's neck. Something jarred. The ancient Egyptian dog had a faint ring of flattened hair running around its neck. A mark left by a collar. Only a collar would leave such a ring in the fur. Dogstar wore a collar.

'Is that you, Dogstar, boy?' The hound's ears remained rigid as spear blades and its eyes stared glassily ahead like a stuffed exhibit in a museum. It was charmed; that's why it didn't recognise him. The goddess had said so. He had better not put it at risk. He decided to keep that hound away from danger.

He pointed to the dog nearest the end and paced six paces to an available hole. He pointed. The hound obediently sprang from the hole, giving an eager yelp. It settled in the designated hole. Too late Phillip saw that it, too, had a ring of flattened hair running around its neck.

A quick check of the other hounds confirmed his fears. They all had marks left by collars around their necks. Were they all identical copies of Dogstar?

A current of fear tugged at Phillip. He felt like a

swimmer who suddenly discovers that he has gone far away from the safety of the shore.

The collar couldn't prove anything anyway. He should have remembered. Ancient Egyptians held their dogs on collars and leashes just as dog owners did today. He looked at the hound he had just moved. Is that one Dogstar after all? Have I gone and placed my dog in danger?

It was the jackal man's turn. He scooped up the dice in large brown hands and let them fly.

'A five once again,' the goddess intoned, reading the score shown by the knucklebones. The jackal man pointed to one of his black-faced jackals — not the first, but one further back — and paced out five spaces so that it leapfrogged other jackals. He was moving them up from the back, slowing down Phillip's advance. Phillip hadn't thought of that tactic. He'd remember it.

It was Phillip's turn to throw the dice. Julia was right. It was cunning of them to throw Dogstar into the balance as a distraction. He hesitated. It was hard enough to concentrate on the game without worrying about keeping one of his pieces out of danger. 'Dogstar, where are you?' Phillip whispered under his breath. 'Give me a sign if you can.'

He threw. 'Four.'

'Move quickly, boy.' It was the jackal-headed man. He snarled it through a mask.

Phillip left the board and returned to stand behind his hounds. It didn't seem to help looking into their faces. He must forget about trying to guess which one was Dogstar and simply try to outplay the jackal man. Rattled by his discoveries, he ignored Julia's advice. He decided to send his advance hound further into enemy lines. Once again he moved the front-running hound, separating it even further from the group and taking it closer to the jackal team.

Through a gap in the mask, the jackal-headed man bared long white teeth in a grin. He was pleased that the boy was being rash.

'Perhaps I'll give you a surprise instead,' Phillip thought.

The jackal man took his turn and threw the dice. 'Three.'

A cautious move. The jackal man moved three paces, again leapfrogging one of his own animals.

Phillip scored a six. Recklessly, he raced his hound onwards.

The jackal man scored a six. He chose a jackal from the end of his row, jumping over his own pieces again, slowing his advance.

Luck was with Phillip, it seemed. He rolled a six. He was closing with the jackals now. He needed only a few more rolls like this and he would make his first kill. The jackals crept closer. The hounds raced to join battle, leaping nearer, throw after throw.

It was Phillip's turn. He needed a four to take a jackal. He scored a three. He moved his hound. Now a jackal and a hound were in neighbouring holes, facing each other, growling, their teeth bared. The jackal man rolled a one.

Disaster.

He pointed to his jackal and then at Phillip's leading dog. 'Attack.' The jackal flew out of its hole and took the hound by the throat. The hound exploded in a flash of light.

Phillip brought up some help. He lost a second dog.

The current of despair took Phillip further out from the shore. Soon he would be beyond help.

Then the jackal man faltered. Phillip threw the four he wanted and now one of his hounds went onto the attack. He destroyed a jackal. It disintegrated with a flash like an exploding cracker.

Phillip heard a whoop of delight behind him. Julia was cheering him on. Heartened by his success, Phillip unleashed another battle hound and sent it running towards the enemy. One throw, two throws, three throws, closing in.

The jackal man gave Phillip a hard look of concern. Stung by the loss of one of his jackals, he stepped up his attack. Jackals and hounds closed on each other around the painted battlefield.

Phillip could feel his confidence rising. He could beat this animal-man of the underworld. Forget about Dogstar. He would take his luck, trust in his own skill and pray that Dogstar wasn't a casualty.

Pray.

Perhaps he shouldn't trust in his own skill alone. He should ask for help. The jackal-headed man made a move. Distracted, Phillip did not notice which piece he had moved.

Concentrate.

We are not alone. Magic has no power over me. I have another power. As he thought it, one of the hounds twisted its head to look at him and it whined fretfully. Dogstar?

He left the hound where it was and chose another, sending it into battle. It also turned to look at him and whined. They were trying to distract him again. Phillip pressed his attack. He rolled a six. He slipped one hound into safety in the enemy's home base. The jackal man did the same, bringing a jackal to safety on Phillip's side.

Phillip now had to choose with his next throw. Did he send this one into safety in the enemy's home base? Or attack?

He paced, thinking. His hand touched the collar in his pocket. He had to win, not strike a draw. He rolled the dice again and moved. A jackal gave a yelp and exploded into dust as one of Phillip's hounds made another kill. The jackal man threw the knucklebones and fell short. Phillip threw again, making another kill.

The jackal man had one jackal running free on the board. Phillip had one hound still vulnerable. They closed on each other like duellists.

Phillip threw a four and pointed to his hound. The hound looked up into his face and, as it lifted its head exposing its neck, Phillip knew something with certainty. This was Dogstar.

Ancient Egyptians may have used collars and leashes, but four thousand years ago they didn't wear municipal registration tags, circular badges of plastic clipped over their collars. There on the dog's neck he saw a faint, circular imprint in the animal's fur. It could only have been left by a dog tag.

'Dogstar, it's you. I know it's you, boy. I know you probably don't understand, but I'm here to save you.'

'Play,' the goddess of the hour said in a sharp tone. If he threw any number larger than two he would place Dogstar within range of an enemy jackal.

He threw. It was a three. The current pulled him under. He had put the pharaoh hound in deadly danger. His throat closed and he dared not breathe as the jackal man, smiling wolfishly, picked up the knuck-lebones, blew on them, then tossed them high into the air.

10

Third hour of night

DID THE JACKAL MAN know how the knucklebones would land? The scene on the brightly lit game board slowed like a videotape image on slow-action replay, one frame at a time passing in front of Phillip's eyes. He saw the first knucklebone land on the board. It was a one.

The second bone followed slowly. Another one. The third, still high in the air, began to twist as if under the power of the jackal man. The 'one' turned uppermost. It was going to be a 'one', a 'one' that could kill Dogstar.

'Catch the bone, 'Star boy,' Phillip said in an urgent whisper.

Dogstar would break out of a dead sleep to catch a flying bone because he was a pharaoh hound and was built for speed and his muscles were spring-loaded for action. The pharaoh hound did it now, taking the bone in midair before it touched the painted board.

'Okay, throw it away, boy.' It knew another trick. The pharaoh hound gave a twist of its head and the knuckle-bone sailed up again. It hit the board and showed a two.

The jackal man gave a cry of protest. He turned to the referee for support. The sky goddess was unmoved.

'The bone cannot score until it lands on the board,' she gave her ruling.

'But the boy intervened.'

'The hound intervened. There is nothing in the rules about the hounds or the jackals intervening.'

'But the hound was supposed to be charmed.'

'I think he is — by the love of a young master. Move your piece, Jackal-Headed One.'

The jackal-headed man pointed to the spot behind Dogstar, leapfrogging harmlessly over the dog's head, missing his hole.

Phillip threw the dice. Julia gave a squeal of delight. He had thrown the right number to bring the pharaoh hound into home base. Phillip had won the game.

'The boy wins!' the goddess declared.

At this, the jackal man threw back his head and howled like a wolf at the moon. Dogstar leapt out of its hole and jumped up at Phillip, its paws on his chest. He gave Phillip the greatest licking of his life. Phillip threw his arms around the animal and gave it a hug.

From the corner of his eye he saw Julia smiling happily and blinking back tears at the same time. He felt the warmth of the dog spreading through his clothing to his body like new strength and encouragement.

It was over. He just wanted to go home with his dog — forget the magical scroll, forget the vanishing past, forget ancient history. They didn't matter. He had his dog back. Wasn't that what he'd come for?

His mission was accomplished.

Then the nightmare returned. Dogstar began to fade.

'No, Dogstar, come back!'

The dog whined. It faded until it was just a collection of glowing atoms. It disappeared.

Phillip's arms were empty.

So was his life.

'You may pass through the gateway to the next hour,' the goddess said.

Nobody seemed to listen or care.

Mist on the river crept on board the pyramid boat. Phillip and Julia sat apart on the deck. Phillip was numb. Why had he been given Dogstar only to have it taken back again? 'Do you know how good it was to hold my dog again?' he said.

'I heard a lovely saying about reunions, that every sad parting is a foretaste of our own deaths, but every joyful reunion is a foretaste of our eternal lives and the joy to come.'

Phillip wondered what that joy might be like if the joy he had felt was only a taste of what was to come. Would he have another chance to rescue Dogstar?

He wondered how he could face the challenges that might lie ahead. More gateways. More monsters. Then what? The hidden room of the deckhouse and its unknown terrors? He wondered whether he should keep trying or simply give up. His fingers touched the ring of Dogstar's collar in his pocket. He remembered his vow. He would keep going. The mist grew thicker.

'This is the realm of Osiris,' the ferryman told them in a dread-filled voice. 'Do not look left or right for here judgment is passed and the wicked are punished in pools of fire and their shadows hacked on execution blocks. Instead, gaze straight ahead and stop your ears with your hands so that the cries of the damned do not drive you from your senses.'

They did as the ferryman instructed. Even so, Phillip heard the howls through his hands. It was worse than the howling of the defeated jackal. He pressed his hands harder against his ears. The crying faded. Phillip took his hands from his ears. The others did the same. The sounds had died to a low moan like a wind. Mist thickened on the water.

The pyramid boat's slender, golden prow, bent like an archer's bow, sliced through the mist to approach the gate of the fourth hour of the underworld night.

Another high dam wall rose out of the gloom, or so it seemed to Phillip — until the walls suddenly moved and began to close around them, walls with muscles and sinews of living rock, limbs with paws that ended in boulder-sized claws. It was not a dam wall, but the outstretched paws of a stone monster. The mountain-sized body and head of a sphinx reared out of the water to challenge them with empty-socket eyes like caves.

Phillip recognised the face. It was an underworld counterpart, immensely magnified, of the sphinx at Giza. It had a pharaoh's head and wore the *nemes* triangular headdress like the sphinx at Giza, but, unlike the famous monument which had lips spread in an enigmatic smile, this creature's mouth was a jagged split of anger like the crack made by an earthquake.

A voice like a crashing hillside made the surface of the underworld river shiver into wavelets. The tomb travellers cowered behind the deckhouse for cover. Phillip peeped.

'I am the Great Sphinx, a god of death, and I shall crush your boat to splinters between my stone paws unless you can answer my riddle.'

'Your turn, Willard,' Barry Coomber said, giving Willard a push from behind, but staying hidden from the terrible face.

'Who will answer the riddle of the Great Sphinx?' the lion-mountain said in a voice that beat down on the tomb travellers like a thousand diorite mallets ringing against stone in a quarry.

'This isn't good, but I'll have a shot at it,' Willard Chase said, going past Phillip towards the sheer rise of the prow.

'Wait, Willard, I think I can help you with the answer,' Phillip whispered.

'But he hasn't asked the riddle yet.'

'No, but I think I can guess what it'll be. I'll bet it's the same riddle the legendary Greek Sphinx used to ask travellers entering Thebes. He asked this: "What goes on four legs in the morning, on two legs at noon and on three legs in the evening?" The Sphinx killed travellers who got the answer wrong. The right answer was "man".' Phillip quickly explained. 'Man crawls on all fours as a baby in the morning of his life, he walks on two legs as a man in the noon of his life and he walks on three legs — with the help of a stick — as an old man in the evening of his life.'

'Thanks, Phillip,' Willard said, 'but we're not supposed to help each other during tests. You'll get me disqualified. I hope you don't do this during school exams.'

The mouth of the sphinx spread in a bitter smile and it laughed as harshly as shale rattling around in a cement mixer. A shower of huge stones fell off its face into the water, making their boat rock dangerously. 'You are mistaken if you think I will use that old riddle. I have a new riddle for you.'

'Why? Stick to tradition,' Willard advised the creature. 'Personally, I like old jokes and riddles.'

'You will answer my new riddle!' it said, flexing the stone muscles in its paws and dashing waves against the side of the sunboat.

'Fire away.'

'Listen well. A king of Egypt voyaged twelve hours west in his royal barque, then he turned around and voyaged twelve hours east, yet he still found himself in the west. What colour were the king's clothes?'

Willard scratched his chin.

'What kind of question is that?' Barry Coomber muttered behind Phillip. 'How are we supposed to know what he was wearing? Was it hot? Maybe he took his clothes off. Maybe he was wearing board shorts and sunglasses. Who knows?'

'It seems unrelated, but there must be an answer hidden in the information,' Julia said, her clever, game-playing mind busily sifting the clues.

'How can the direction in which he sailed have anything to do with his clothes? It's a nonsense riddle,' Coomber said.

'Twelve hours west,' Julia said, thinking aloud. 'Twelve hours east. Strange directions.'

'Very strange directions,' Phillip said, agreeing with her. 'A king voyaging on the river Nile in Egypt couldn't travel very far in the direction of west or east, except briefly during a bend in the river, and certainly not for a period of twelve hours.'

'I think that's the clue,' Julia said. 'There's another riddle like it. It goes like this: a bear walked one kilometre south, then it turned and walked one kilometre east. Then it turned again and walked one kilometre north. It wound up right back where it started. What colour was the bear?'

'That's also a dumb, nonsense riddle,' Coomber said.

'No, it's not. The directions give it away. The directions tell you what part of the world the bear lived in. To go south a kilometre, east a kilometre and north a kilometre and then to end up where it started, the bear had to be at the north pole. So the bear was white. It was a *polar* bear.'

'But we know what part of the world the king was in. He was a king of Egypt. So he was on the Nile — or was he? Maybe he was at sea. No, that still wouldn't make sense.' Coomber shrugged. 'Where in the world was he?'

'Maybe he wasn't in the world at all,' Phillip said, guessing the answer.

'Give your answer,' the sphinx boomed at Willard Chase.

Willard cleared his throat. Phillip tensed. Should he creep forward and whisper the answer to Willard? Dare he risk it? The sphinx had heard his whisper earlier. Would he disqualify Willard and bring the lion-mountain falling on top of them in anger?

'I have the answer, Great Sphinx.'

'Many have failed and perished.'

'I'll take that risk.' Willard was an archaeological detective. He would know.

'Then answer.'

'I think I know the answer,' Julia whispered.

'Well, I don't,' Coomber said.

'Sh-sh,' Phillip said.

'Here's my answer. If a king of Egypt journeyed in his royal barque in the way that you described,' Willard said, 'then he was certainly dressed in white clothes. Wrappings, you see. He was dressed as a mummy because he was dead. *That's* why he still found himself in the west. The west is the Egyptian land of the dead.

'He travelled twelve hours from east to west in the sun barque, then twelve hours from west to east in the night barque, but remained in the west. Therefore the king voyaged in the land of the blessed and was dressed in white grave clothes.'

At this, the head of the sphinx blew off its shoulders like the top off an exploding volcano. Flame and molten rock lit up the underworld sky. The sphinx's massive paws, flexing in a last impulse, turned red and sank with a bubbling hiss into the river. Smoke hung over the spot.

The smoke was all that stood between them and the fourth hour of the night.

11

The kingdom of death

IN THE PROVINCE OF THE FOURTH hour of night, the ferryman moored the pyramid boat on the riverbank.

'Why have we stopped here, Herhaf?' Phillip asked. 'We must press ahead. We mustn't stop now and look over our shoulders, but keep our eyes fixed straight ahead.'

'That is easy for you to say, forward boy. Your head is not twisted to face backwards as mine is. We have entered the kingdom of death, the realm of Seker, which is shaped like a pyramid, a realm of rocks and mountains and winged serpents with two and three heads and other soul-devouring monsters. None may pass by river here, not even pharaohs, although I may do so, being of this world.'

He pointed, swinging his arm behind his back. 'Do you see those glows in the dark? They are torches of perpetual flame. Follow them, collecting them as you go to provide light. You will come to the entrance to a great pyramid.

'Follow the passage cut out of the rock for a period of two hours and it will take you above the terrible kingdom of death. I will take the boat through two more gateways and will be waiting for you at the entrance to the seventh hour, but you will have only two hours in which to rejoin the boat, so make all speed.

'Be warned, however, that if you are not at the gate at the appointed hour, the sun barque must proceed without you and you must remain in the kingdom of death forever.'

'Let's not stand around talking,' Phillip said. 'Let's run.'

The crew of shades put out a gang-plank and the tomb travellers went ashore.

It was good to feel firm ground underfoot again, Phillip thought, as he ran along the river bank. There were no reeds here; just hard ground and scattered stones.

'There are the lamps up ahead,' Willard said. He took the first one and Phillip, Coomber and Julia each took the rest in turn. By the time Julia took hers they had reached a deeper square of shadow at the base of a soaring black pyramid.

'I'll lead the way,' Willard said.

'Do you think that's a good idea?' Phillip said.

'Yeah, we've only got two hours,' Coomber said caustically. 'We can't afford to get lost.'

'Questioning my sense of direction, are you?' Willard said, pretending to be indignant. 'Very wise. You go first, Phillip.' He stood aside.

Phillip set off along a corridor cut out of the stone, the others following close behind. The sound of their footsteps rang in the narrow passage and the flames of their torches threw twisting shadows like hands reaching out to slow them.

There were no wall paintings to enliven the passageway, no marching lines of hieroglyphs to cheer them with the thought that at least once, communicating souls had tried to leave their mark.

Phillip stretched his muscles willingly after the confinement of the boat journey. The blood began to race around his body and his heart pounded like his feet hitting the stone. They were making progress, working their way through the pyramid of the kingdom of death to safety on the other side.

They came to crossroads in the corridors. They stopped. 'Which way now?' They glanced in all four directions.

'There's a stela lying on the floor,' Willard Chase said, pointing to a stone pillar.

They gathered around it, illuminating its stone surfaces with the light of their torches. Willard lifted it onto its base and circled it, examining each surface. It was four-sided with different signs carved on each surface. 'It's a signpost, each face pointing to a different route. Unfortunately, it's fallen over, or been pushed aside, so we don't know which way it's supposed to be orientated.' On one side it showed a symbol of Osiris in the form of a mummified man, on another Seker in the form of a mummified falcon, on the third side a serpent and on the last side a beetle.

'That's a lot of help,' Coomber complained. 'How are we supposed to figure that out?'

'We've got to be quick,' Phillip said. 'We've only got two hours and we don't know how far we still have to go. We don't want the boat to leave without us.'

Willard looked helpless. 'We could trust in my sense of direction,' he said.

'There has to be a better way.'

'There is,' Julia said. 'There's a simple answer to this puzzle. Where are we going at the moment?'

'Through the land of Seker,' Willard said. 'That'll be this carving here of the mummified falcon.'

'What's the good of knowing that?' Coomber said. 'We don't know which way this signpost's supposed to be pointing. It's fallen over.'

'So we're going through the land of Seker,' Julia said, repeating what Willard had said. 'Fine. Now where have we come from?'

'From the realm of Osiris.' Willard pointed. 'Here's the symbol on this side.'

'Then the answer's simple,' the bright-eyed girl said, laughing at their puzzled looks. 'We simply turn the post so that the sign of Osiris points down the way we've just come. We may not know which way to go, but we do know which passage we've come along. Get that right and we know the signpost is set in the correct way.'

'Well done, Jool,' Phillip said, giving her a hug. 'I'm glad I brought you along.'

'Yes, thanks a lot, Phillip.'

They ran on.

The passage they were following blew out into a cavernous, enclosed hall with a roof that was lost in darkness. They stopped at the edge of a drop. They found themselves at the brink of a square-shaped moat surrounding a temple. The moat had long since dried up. Living liquid had taken the place of water in the moat. Snakes and scorpions flowed in slow-moving, oily currents beneath the travellers.

'Swim anybody?' Willard said.

'Very funny,' Julia said. The square-shaped moat blocked the way to a pyloned temple that revealed an open doorway. There was no other way out of the hall, except through that doorway. But how did they cross the moat to reach the temple entrance?

Baffled, they walked around the edge of the moat. Barry Coomber tripped over a couple of planks.

'I think I just discovered a way over,' he said, picking up one of the planks. 'This should do it.' He went to the edge of the moat and held out the plank. He wobbled at the brink with the weight of the extended plank. Willard had to steady him.

Coomber tried again, stretching to reach the far side, but the plank fell several centimetres short. It missed the brink and fell into the gap, almost dragging Coomber with it. He barely managed to keep hold of the plank. Coomber found himself staring down into a slow-moving whirlpool of reptiles and scorpions. Willard hooked an arm around Coomber's waist, pulling him back.

'Let's try the other plank,' Coomber said, disappointed. He put down the plank and picked up the new one and was about to dangle it over the edge of the moat again when Julia burst out laughing.

'You men are so unpractical. Just put it against the first plank and see if it's longer.'

Coomber wasn't grateful for her suggestion. He gave her a glare, but followed her suggestion, laying the second plank on top of the first. They were identical lengths.

'Perfect,' Coomber said sarcastically. 'Maybe the moat is narrower in one spot.' He made a tour of the moat and returned shaking his head. 'No luck. There's only one thing for it. We'll have to nail them together.'

'There are no nails and there's no hammer,' Julia pointed out.

'Oh.'

'Maybe we could make a springboard,' Willard suggested. 'We could rest one board on the other and hold the end down while we take it in turn to jump.'

'That's fine, but what about the last person to go?' Phillip said.

'That's no problem. It can be you,' Coomber said.

'Stop arguing; we're wasting time,' Julia said wearily. 'Simply put one plank across a corner of the moat, then run the second plank from it like an upside down 'T'. You'll find it stretches easily to the far side of the moat. Simple. You boys aren't much good with shapes. You've obviously never had to cut out a dress pattern.'

Phillip and Willard looked at her in wonder, Coomber with a flash of resentment. 'I hate smart girls,' he said.

They did as Julia suggested and it worked, making a T-shaped bridge across the moat. They went over one at a time. The wood creaked under Coomber and gave a loud crack under Willard, but they made it across. Phillip went first into the temple doorway. It led to stairs that took them down to a passage on a lower level. They began to descend; maybe the exit wasn't far away, Phillip thought. He wondered how far they had come. Was the pyramid boat already waiting for them at the next gate?

The passage widened into a vault-shaped chamber like the king's chamber in the great pyramid, but unlike the king's chamber it was empty. Looking ahead, Phillip saw that the passage continued beyond the chamber.

That's when he saw the blur of a moving figure in the passage. It looked like a mummy with a bird's head.

Seker.

It pulled a lever and a giant stone portcullis rumbled down with a floor-jarring crash, sealing the way out of the king's chamber. They turned to run back and now another stone portcullis grated shut behind them. They were locked in the heart of the pyramid, trapped under tonnes of stone.

'There's a lever on the other side of the stone block,' Phillip told them. 'I saw someone push it.'

'Someone?'

'Something.'

'This isn't good,' Willard said.

Things couldn't be worse, Phillip thought; but he changed his mind when the stone roof of the chamber, a solid block of granite, slowly began to descend on them.

'Does anybody have any ideas?' Willard said.

'Yeah, anybody,' Coomber said, looking hopefully at Julia, 'even you.'

'I thought you hated smart girls. Don't look at me. I can't see a way out of this.'

'There may be a ventilation shaft,' Willard said hopefully, 'if it's anything like the Great Pyramid.'

'There is,' Coomber said. He pointed to a small black square in the wall angling diagonally upwards.

Their excitement tumbled when they took a closer look. It was a narrow square, barely offering crawling space. It would never take their bodies, at least not those of Willard and Coomber. They looked at Julia again.

'Will you stop looking at me? I couldn't crawl into that. I'd panic in a closed space.'

The ceiling of stone crept down.

'Then I'll try,' Phillip said. He was the smallest, after Julia. 'Help me up, Willard.'

Willard crouched and Phillip climbed on his shoulders. Willard straightened, raising him to the level of the shaft. 'A few tips. I've been in some tight spaces,' Willard said. 'You've got to pour yourself through. Don't tense, whatever you do. Think of yourself as a snake. Wriggle minutely, moving your muscles forward in waves. It's called "reptation".'

Phillip fitted his shoulders to the hole and crawled inside on his stomach. 'Hurry up, Phillip! The roof's getting awfully low!' Julia said.

The stone sweated. In some places it was hard and brittle, in others it was like slime. He felt the moisture seep through his clothes to his skin. Where was the mummy figure? Would it be waiting for him at the end of his crawl or had it already blocked the vent, sealing Phillip inside a stone gullet?

The passage narrowed still further, making him wriggle in a snake-like motion to clear it. The shaft was tight, oval-shaped, hampering. In places it throttled almost too tightly to let his shoulders through. To get through these difficult spots he blew the air from his lungs, changing his body like a bubble to make use of every inch of space in order to fit himself to the tube; then the only way to move was to wriggle his body in tiny movements.

Phillip tried not to think about sticking now, when he could feel the squeeze of the stone around his shoulders and rib cage and the stirring of panic, an unpleasant tickle in his lungs, urging him to fill his lungs with air. But when he tried to take in more air, he felt his ribs meet unsqueezable stone, so he kept moving and blew out the air, compressing his ribs even more because stone wouldn't give and his body would.

It was when he made one final effort to get through with no air in his lungs at all and *still* couldn't do it, but became jammed tighter, that he knew what it was to be afraid.

Fright bunched his muscles, jamming him tightly against the stone, so tightly that hope fled from him that he would ever be free again. His body was just too big for the place it filled; there was no room to go on. He inched back into a wider spot, where he rested.

He had failed. He listened. He could hear the grating sound of the stone roof descending in the chamber behind him. At any moment it would reach Willard and Coomber and Julia, crushing them. He couldn't fail them. He must try again.

He edged back into the tight place.

In between the waves of panic that ran down his sweating body, a memory raised its hand like a drowning swimmer signalling for help. He remembered what Willard had said. 'Don't tense, whatever you do. Think of yourself as a snake. Wriggle minutely, moving your muscles forward in waves. It's called "reptation".'

The thought calmed him. He sipped air rather than trying to fill his lungs. He stuck again, but this time he knew what he needed to do. Before he could break the grip of the stone, he had to break the grip of fright on his muscles. He stroked his fears in the darkness and spoke to his muscles one at a time.

Get down, shoulder muscles. Get down, chest muscles. Get down, leg muscles. His body worked itself free and he moved on, like a snake, on waves of rolling muscles.

The passage widened and corkscrewed around and down. It was taking him back to the other end of the passage. He dropped like a letter through a letter box into the passage. He found himself in impenetrable darkness.

He could hear the rumbling sound of the roof coming down on the travellers, muffled by the stone portcullis that blocked their escape, and he groped towards it. He stumbled into a lever. He heard a muffled scream pierce the stone, then he hauled back on the lever.

The portcullis lifted and light stabbed his eyes. Julia, Willard and Coomber were lying flat on the floor of the chamber, still holding their torches, with the roof pressing against their backs, but now, blessedly, the roof lifted.

'Thanks for taking so long,' Coomber said in a complaining voice. 'Did you go off exploring somewhere?'

'Why complain?' Willard said — and then quipped: 'Our clothes needed a press.'

The tomb travellers ran out of the passage and found themselves once again in a stony desert.

The pyramid boat was waiting for them at the entrance to the seventh hour of night and they were allowed to sail through the pylons and into the seventh hour of night.

12

Seventh hour of night

THE SEVENTH SECTION of underworld night was a realm of swamps and shallows. 'This is the realm of Apep, the serpent,' the ferryman told them. 'It is a monster seventy cubits long.'

Julia saw it lying on a sandbank. It was gold with black markings and it lay on a sandbank that was several hundred metres wide. Its head was lost in clumps of marshy reeds.

'Let's give it a wide berth,' Willard said to the helmsman.

'We cannot. We may not pass until we have over-powered it. One of you must fight the serpent.'

'Fight it!' Coomber said, goggling over the side of the boat. 'It's as long as a city block. How can anybody fight it?'

'With this,' Herhaf said, taking a knife with a feather-shaped blade out of the inside of his white *galabia*. 'You must fight him to prevent him from crushing and swallowing you.'

'With that penknife! I wouldn't get on that sandbank if you gave me a missile launcher.'

'One of you must face Apep. Who will it be?'

'I think it's a job for Willard,' Coomber said.

'That's nice,' Julia said. 'What about you?'

'On second thoughts, maybe it should be you, Julia. Serpents and dragons always prefer eating maidens. Maybe you could pacify it. Teach it to play snakes and ladders.' Julia looked ready to push him over the side.

'Why don't I volunteer?' Willard said, taking the knife from Herhaf.

'I'll put you onto the sandbank,' Herhaf said, turning the steering oar.

'What advice can you give me?' Willard asked the ferryman.

'Only this. Do not let it crush and swallow you.'

'That's your advice?'

'It's the best advice of all. Do this and you will survive, I assure you.'

'Hm.'

'What are you going to do, Willard?' Phillip said.

'Nothing,' he said. 'Absolutely nothing. I want you all to make me a promise. Whatever seems to be happening, however bad things may look, stay where you are and don't get involved. Do you hear?'

They nodded.

'Good luck, Willard,' Julia said, looking pale.

'It's been nice knowing you,' Coomber said.

'Not so sure I can say the same about you,' Willard muttered.

The ferryman guided the pyramid boat to the edge of the sandbank and Willard climbed over the side and gingerly tested the sand with the toe of a desert boot.

It gave a little, yet took his weight. It wasn't quicksand. He jumped down and cautiously approached the serpent.

The serpent ignored him. Perhaps it wasn't a snake at all, but a stretch of abandoned pipeline from an oil refinery that had fallen down from the real world into this infernal place. No, it was a snake all right, Phillip thought. He could see the scales. It wore a chain mail of golden scales, each scale the size of a saucer.

Willard went unmolested to the snake, raised the knife over his head and struck hard at its side. Clank. A spark flew off the blade. It sounded like metal hitting metal. The snake convulsed, throwing a curving wave along the length of its body. The travelling shock wave of scales hit Willard with force, throwing him flat on the sand.

He lay motionless on his back with his arms flung open and his feet together like a human cross, the blade still in his hand. The serpent's head reared from its hiding place in the marshy reeds and it turned like a monorail train on a curve, streaming towards the fallen man.

'The serpent's knocked him cold,' Coomber said. 'That's the end of him.'

'I'll take an oar and hit it!' Julia said fiercely.

'No,' Phillip said. 'Remember Willard's instructions. Whatever happens, however bad things look, don't get involved.' Julia sank her face into Phillip's shoulder, daring only to watch with one eye.

The serpent, tongue flickering like lightning, tested the air, sizing up its prey. Willard lay motionless as a tree stump. The serpent's head, the size of a small car, descended to the level of the sand. It gave Willard an exploratory nudge with its nose. It was a light nudge, but it shifted Willard's body along the sand. He did not stir, nor did he change the attitude of his body.

The snake began its meal. It went for the head first as snakes will, and seemed about to swallow him, but it noticed Willard's outflung arms. They could cause a dangerous obstruction. It went next to his feet which were tightly clamped together. This seemed easier.

Phillip, Julia and Coomber watched, chilled, as the serpent prepared to swallow Willard Chase. It opened its mouth like the hinged lid of a car bonnet and took first his boots into the pink cave, then the ankles and the knees. 'I'm going to be sick,' Julia said.

Still Willard did not move. His body was disappearing into the swallowing-tube of scales. It reached Willard's thighs. Now it unhinged its jaws to take in the greater width of hips and upper body. It was a critical stage for the snake. A snake halfway through a meal was at its most vulnerable. Willard's thighs and now his hips vanished into the tube.

When it was at his waist and its meal was half-swallowed, Willard moved. He arched forward, slid the blade into a corner of the serpent's unhinged mouth and slit it down like the side of a sack. Then he swung to the other corner and slit that, too. With jaws unhinged, the serpent was powerless to bite. Willard flung back the monster's head. It rolled back like a fleshy flap.

He crawled out of the serpent. The serpent tried to hold him with its lightning-fork tongue, wrapping it wetly around the ankle of his boot. Willard slashed at it with the knife.

The serpent, as useless as a broken bag, thrashed

and writhed, flapping the two halves of its head and neck. Willard ran to the safety of the boat where eager hands pulled him aboard.

13

Eighth hour of night

THEY PASSED FREELY and without incident through the gateway of the eighth hour of the underworld night. The challenge came in the hour itself when a hippopotamus reared out of the waters like a surfacing island, sending waves rolling against the prow of the boat. The hippo opened its cavernous mouth to roar, white water streaming from its teeth.

As the giant creature rose higher in the water, an extraordinary fact emerged. The hippopotamus was the colour of blue-glazed pottery and its hide was decorated with motifs of marsh plants and lotus flowers sketched in black outline. 'This is crazy, but I know that hippopotamus!' Phillip said. 'I even know its name. William.'

'William?' Julia said, eyeing the beast dubiously.

'I've seen its picture in books.'

'I've seen the real William,' Willard Chase said. 'I've been to William's home. The Metropolitan Museum of Art in New York.'

'What are you two talking about?' Julia said. 'How can an ancient Egyptian hippo have a name like William?'

'It's a nickname. William is one of the museum's most famous exhibits and a favourite with visitors. He's made of pottery, glazed in brilliant blue faïence, and the largest and most exquisite example of its kind from Egypt's Middle Kingdom period.

'An article appeared about him in *Punch* back in the thirties. A certain captain owned a colour print of the hippo which took pride of place in the family living room. It came to be regarded as an oracle. It seemed that William, as the family called him, reacted to the family's fortunes. He could wear different expressions, either kindly or forbidding, depending on whether he favoured the family's plans. The name William stuck.'

'Let's hope William's lucky for us,' Julia said.

'Don't be too sure,' Willard said. 'The hippo, while revered by the ancient Egyptians and placated with offerings, was seen as a symbol of the perverse forces in the world.'

'He's looking pretty perverse right now,' Julia said.

'What does he want of us?' Willard asked the ferryman.

'He has risen to challenge you,' the man whose face is turned backwards said. 'One of you must play a game against him.'

'What game can you play against a hippo?' Julia said.

'A water game, naturally,' the ferryman said. 'What else?'

'I wouldn't get into the water with that thing,' Coomber said. 'He could snap a boat in half with his jaws.'

'The game is called "war galleons",' Herhaf said. 'It will be a naval battle between the creature's fleet and our single boat.'

'That doesn't sound very fair,' Julia said. 'One boat against a whole fleet. How many boats does he have?'

'Nine war galleons. But it is an advantage for us having only one boat. It is harder for him to hit you. The idea is to fire across a wall at each other's ships — and to destroy each other.'

'I know the game. It's battleships!' Julia said, identifying the game instantly. 'I'll play him.'

Coomber looked sceptical. 'Battleships is a boys' game. You'd be no good at it.'

'That's what I thought once,' Phillip said, remembering how Julia had beaten him at the video war game. 'But I think differently now. As long as it's a game, Julia will have an unfair advantage.'

'You're going to let her play a boys' game?'

'Too right I am.'

'That's dumb. I'll play the game,' Coomber said, a confident gleam in his eye. 'I'm pretty good at battleships.'

'Julia's not just good — she's special. At any game.'

'I'll put my faith in her,' Willard said. 'I haven't forgotten her inspired match against the great ape on our last journey. Let Julia play.'

'But this isn't chess.'

'Let her play,' Phillip said firmly.

Coomber looked from Phillip to Willard, wondering whether to defy them both, then he shrugged. 'Don't blame me if she fails and we're stuck here. It's no time to be polite to girls.' Julia ignored his remark and went calmly to the prow.

The hippo spoke. 'You will challenge me, little girl? Isn't there a man among you? This is a war game!'

'Don't you call me a little girl, you fat old piggy bank. You want a game; I'll give it to you. Now how do we play?'

'Look down at the water.' They looked down. A grid made of thin black lines appeared on the water, turning it into a gameboard with squares. Along the horizontal of the grid were letters of the alphabet; on the vertical side were the numbers.

'Now look behind me.' A fleet of war galleys rowed by oarsmen crept into view onto the hippo's water grid. 'I shall station my war galleons strategically on the board and you must guess where they are. We shall take it in turn to fire.'

'Fire with what?' asked Julia. 'I don't have a pencil and paper.'

'What is a pencil?'

'A thing for writing with.'

'You mean a pen and papyrus? We do not play this game on paper, little girl; we play it with missiles of stone.'

'I don't have a missile of stone.'

'The sky goddess will provide them. Prepare to fight. You may fire the first shot. Choose your shot and call it by the grid.'

'Not so fast,' Julia said. 'What about the rules?' Julia was a stickler for the rules. 'How many squares do your war galleons occupy?'

'One, the same as your boat,' the shiny blue hippo said.

'Are your boats allowed to be placed on touching squares?'

'No.'

'Not even diagonally?'

'Not even diagonally.'

'Can we move our boat?'

'When the wall comes up, you may move anywhere you like — but my missiles of stone will find you. You must sink all of my fleet within the hour — if you want to survive.'

The blue hippo raised his head and sang in a humorous, wallowy voice:

Mark the ships you see;
You'll search in vain for me.
My ships I'll move but three,
Yet I'll turn my fleet to flee.

He sank back into the water, a secretive smile on his granite-block muzzle.

'I hope his aim is as bad as his singing,' Julia said, sweeping the hippo's fleet with a gaze. The hippo's fighting ships were arranged in a triangular formation, the apex thrust aggressively forward. Her view of them was soon lost. Out of the river, a wall of stone arose, spilling water over its broad top like a dam in flood, blocking the hippo and his fleet from view.

The goddess of the hour came onto the wall and, following her, a vast engine of war — some sort of catapult — dragged by giants. Behind them came more giants dragging a sled stacked with boulders. Between them they lifted a boulder up to the engine, loading it into a leather sling at the end of the catapult's arm.

Was the hippo arranging his fleet? Julia wisely de-cided to do the same. 'Move our boat so it lies at J-5,' she said. Phillip relayed her instructions to the ferryman. The rowers moved them forward and Her-haf guided them into position. The unseen crew of shades dropped anchor.

The lady of the hour turned to point to their sunboat. She spoke to them. Again her voice seemed to spiral down from the stars. 'The battle of the galleons will commence. Choose your first shot, child.'

'Remember, if you miss, the hippo gets a shot at us,' Phillip whispered.

'He's got a whole fleet, but we've only got one boat, so be careful.'

With a mind strengthened by a thousand successful chess contests, Julia had learnt to commit an opponent's game to memory. She would see the hippo's grid and all the ships on it exactly as it had been, as clearly as if it were still before her. But where had he moved his ships?

Phillip could imagine her thoughts. The words of the hippo's song were some kind of clue. She would be running the words through her mind line by line.

'Mark the ships you see. . .' She would certainly have done that already. 'You'll search in vain for me.' A boast? But the next line: 'My ships I'll move but three. . .' What did that mean? Had William moved all of his ships but three? Or moved only three? 'Yet I'll turn my fleet to flee. . .' How could moving just three ships turn his whole fleet around?

'E-10', Julia called.

The engine of war convulsed and a ball like a planet flew up from the wall in a graceful parabola. The lady on the wall pointed and seemed to guide its fall. It passed from view over the far side of the wall to hit the river. A spout of water rose higher than the wall.

'A miss,' the lady called.

'Now we can look out,' Coomber said. 'Did you see the size of that boulder?' The ferryman tightened his grip on the steering oar as if to brace himself. 'Our 4600-year-old timbers will not take a hit and remain afloat,' he warned them.

Willard and Phillip exchanged anxious looks. The catapult fired.

'Here it comes!' Coomber said, ducking. Phillip watched the boulder's arc. The lady on the wall pointed. The boulder fell three squares away from their boat, yet the wave it threw up dashed against their sides and lifted their flat-bottomed hull.

'I thought we were sunk,' Coomber said.

It was Julia's turn again. Her face was calm, composed by a cool deadliness of purpose. Phillip had seen her like this before. In a game, Julia became another person. The printed circuit of her mind entertained no more idea of mercy than a computer. She went about sweetly destroying her opponents and did not relax until victory. Julia was a good person to have on your side, he thought admiringly. He hoped he would never have to face her in a contest.

She closed her eyes to picture the formation of the fleet she had seen. 'H-4.'

The catapult cracked and another asteroid-like missile flew. Another miss. The ferryman muttered under his breath.

They waited for the hippo's response. It soon came. The catapult lurched on the wall. A missile sailed into the air and hit the infernal river with a boom like a mine going off, almost turning them over. It fell two squares away.

'He knows where we are!' Phillip said. 'Julia, please hit something — before he hits us!'

The ferryman shook his backward-facing head. 'He is a creature of the water and he can feel our position just as a fish feels the presence of another by waves of pressure.'

'Fire again, child,' the sky goddess instructed Julia. 'B-4,' she said. The giants had already reloaded. They fired. Their hearts fell with the shot. No crash of splint-ering wood greeted their ears, just a splash of water.

'A miss.'

'Duck,' Barry Coomber said. 'We're going to get it this time.'

The engine on the wall released its next missile. The boulder sailed up from the wall and grew in the sky over the pyramid boat. It sped towards them. 'He's got us pinned.'

It hit with the explosion of a depth charge. It missed their boat, but it might just as well have hit. The shock wave twisted their boat and drew shrieks of complaint from its ancient timbers. The pyramid boat lurched out of the water and bellyflopped heavily. The hippo's shot had landed in an adjoining square of the grid.

'Good,' Julia said, a smile of satisfaction on her face. 'Now I know where he isn't.'

'That may not be enough, Julia. You'd better know where he is.'

'Same thing. He's moved only three ships and now I know which three.'

'He couldn't have moved only three. He said he'd turned his fleet to flee.'

'It's like a trick you can do with nine coins. You

make a triangular shape from nine coins, then change the direction of the triangle completely by moving first the apex then the two outside coins of the base in the other direction. Watch.' She lifted her head and called to the star woman.

'B-8.' The engine of war bucked on its wheels and spewed a missile. The sound of a splintering crash came back over the wall and after that a bellow of rage. The hippo had taken a hit. They cheered. Julia would be allowed another turn, as long as she kept hitting. Phillip crossed his fingers.

'H-8,' she called. The next boulder flew. The sound of another crash and another roar of anger came back over the wall. Willard Chase whooped. Phillip eased out a sigh of relief, but Julia did not relax, although he sensed that she was enjoying herself now.

She directed a stream of deadly shots over the wall: F-8, D-8, C-6, G-6, D-4, F-4. She paused. 'To wrap up the game, I'll try E-2,' she said.

The bellow of the hippo rose to a sustained rumble like thunder. The figures on the wall and the engine of war vanished. The wall descended back into the water. 'We finished him,' Coomber said. They went to the bow post to stare at the wreckage of the hippo's navy. Planks and spars and pieces of *halfa* grass rope festooned the water where his ships had been.

'Nine battleships sunk,' Phillip said in admiration. 'Great shooting, Jool!'

'Not bad for a girl,' Coomber said grudgingly although looking relieved. 'Still, it wasn't too hard — no submarines to worry about.'

'Speaking of submarines,' Willard said pointing at the water. 'Do you see what I see?' A blue underwater island, covered with sketches of lotus flowers and marsh plants, streaked towards their boat, powered by paddling legs.

'He's going to torpedo us!'

'Oh no, he isn't!' Julia said flatly. 'That's absolutely against the rules!'

You couldn't break the rules in a game against Julia. You couldn't even try. Julia was outraged. She jumped onto the bow post and with one arm around it she leaned out over the water and shook her finger at the creature rushing at their hull.

'You stop that cheating right now, William! Submarines aren't allowed! Do you hear?'

The hippo had second thoughts. Its legs stopped powering and it rose, its two outcrops of boulder eyes emerging from the water to peep guiltily at Julia. 'Now stop that!' she said firmly. 'I won't have it! I hate people — or creatures — who don't stick to the rules! So behave!'

The hippo blinked sheepishly. 'The game is over,' she told it, still shaking her finger at it. 'Do you hear?' William twitched its small ears.

What would happen next? Phillip wondered. Would the defeated hippo explode in frustration as the sphinx had done? He hoped not. The hippo was likeable in a clumsy way. William grimaced and gave a long, bubbling grumble under the water as if its multiple ruminant's stomachs were each hit with a spasm of stomach ache at the same time. It turned and swam to the bank. It hauled its bulk ashore and turned fully around to throw one last injured look at Julia.

Hairline cracks like those on ancient pottery rivered all over its body.

William froze where he stood. 'That's exactly the way he looks in the museum,' Willard said. 'Except he isn't smiling. I hope that's not a warning of worse to come.'

14

The hidden room

THE GODDESS OF THE HOUR, a collection of dancing stars in the shape of a woman, appeared at the pyloned gateway of the ninth hour of night.

'You have done well, travellers in the underworld,' she said in her spiralling voice. 'You will face no more monsters from without until you meet the great serpent in the twelfth hour of night. Now as you travel through the next three gateways, you must face the monsters that lurk within.'

'Within what?' Phillip said. 'Do you mean in the hidden room — the deckhouse? Or in ourselves?'

'Both, for the deckhouse is the hidden room of the self. You must go in in turn and, like Horus who leads the dead into judgment, you,' she said, pointing to Phillip, 'must lead the others into the hidden place, since this is your journey into the past.'

'Who must go first?'

'The child of light first, the vile boy next, then you, alone.'

'What about Willard?' Coomber said as if Willard Chase had not been through enough after his nightmarish struggle with the serpent.

'The young ones only.'

'Good — I get to have a rest,' Willard said. 'I think I need it.'

The goddess of the hour opened the gateway and they passed into the ninth hour of night. Julia looked at the deckhouse and swallowed. 'I'm awfully glad you're coming in there with me,' she said to Phillip.

'I'll look after you; don't be afraid. There's nothing in there. Herhaf said so.'

'Can we walk around it first before we go inside?'

He nodded. They slowly circled the structure. The walls were made of a series of light wooden screens. Julia put her ear to one of the screens. 'Nothing,' she said. There was a double door in the forward deck-house and a single door leading to the afterdeck.

Phillip took Julia to the forward door. They went inside and found themselves in an anteroom. Julia took Phillip's hand. Her hand was cold. 'I feel terribly afraid, Phillip,' she said. He gave her hand a reassur-ing squeeze. They went through another door into the main deckhouse area, into a perfumed pool of incense.

A column of light burnt in the middle of the room. The inside of the deckhouse was vastly bigger than it appeared to be on the outside. Columns with palmette capitals held up the roof and the room was wreathed in blue, sweet-smelling smoke.

The column of shining light drew them nearer. 'Look what the light's shining on,' Julia said, her glance falling to the deck. A flat object lay at the base of the column of light like a performer in a spotlight.

'It's a book,' Phillip said.

'Not exactly,' Julia said. 'It's a photo album and not

just any album. It's the one with pictures of my mother and father in it.' It was a blue album, with a brass ring binder at its spine. It was closed. 'It's an illusion, obviously. How else could it be here?'

'Maybe you brought it with you.'

'No I didn't; that's silly.'

'Not physically. In your mind.'

She tore her eyes away from the album. 'What are you saying, Phillip? What's happening? I don't like it here.'

'Remember what the ferryman said about this room? It's the hidden room. Each of us will find something different in the hidden room, according to his need. In the hidden room we will meet our secret fears, the past that we must face.'

'What am I supposed to do?'

'What you're afraid to do.'

She allowed her eyes to travel back to the closed album lying on the deck. 'I'm not opening it.'

They heard a scuttling noise. Julia shrank against Phillip. Out of the blue-wreathed darkness, gleaming metallically like a black, armoured Samurai warrior, came a scorpion, its heavy claws held out as if to grapple with the column of light. It dropped its claws like a set of heavy brackets around the light, guarding the book.

Julia pulled Phillip's arm. 'Let's get out of here.'

He held her back. 'This is one of the tests. You have to face it.'

'What do you mean "face it"? What am I supposed to do?'

'I think it's pretty clear, Julia. You've got to open the book.'

'But I don't want to open the past.'

'You must open the past or we're going to be stuck in it for all eternity.'

'Just open it?'

'Open it and look at the pictures inside.'

'With that thing squatting there? Never. It's shuddersome.'

'It's only a monster of your mind. Forget it and go to the album.'

She sobbed against his chest. 'But I don't want to, Phillip. I've closed that part of my life and I don't want to open it again. It hurts too much.'

'Face it.'

'I can't.'

'You're not alone, remember.'

'I can't do it, even with you here.'

'I don't mean me. Remember the story you told the seekers of light? Hold that story in your mind and you can do it.'

'Do you think so?'

'Yes, Jool. Do it.'

She gulped, letting go of his hand. 'I suppose I must, for all of us.'

'No, for yourself most of all.'

The pigtailed girl let go of his arm and went in small, timid steps towards the pool of light. The black scorpion stirred. The wicked barb of its sting arched over its back, suspended over Julia's head. Julia faltered. The sting arched further, stopping inches away from the nape of Julia's exposed neck, at the pale line of the parting of her hair.

Julia shuddered, but went on into the pool of light. The scorpion's headlamp eyes flickered warningly.

The outspread claws scraped on the floor, closing around the book. Julia knelt on the floor in front of the blue photo album and bent her head to look at the blue cover.

'Open it,' Phillip willed her.

The arching sting of the scorpion followed the nape of her neck. A drop of gleaming venom hung from the point. If Julia pulled back now or even lifted her head a fraction it would sink its sting like a thousand-volt shock of lightning pain. Julia reached out into the pool of light with an unsteady hand and turned the first page.

A sob shook out of her. 'Mother,' she whispered. 'Father.' She turned more pages. 'I don't remember you, yet I've tried to shut you away and forget you. Will you forgive me?' Her shoulders shook again. 'Happy shots. Your wedding day. My christening. Happy families. You, holding me as a baby, smiling proudly, thinking that we would be together forever.' Julia cried, not bitterly, but with gentle acceptance.

It tore at Phillip more than a cry of anguish. He wanted to go to the girl and comfort her, but knew that he mustn't move.

She paged through more of the pages of the album. Her mood changed. She must have reached a funny shot, because she gave a little chuckle. 'You were so cute,' she said. She paged through more photos and chuckled some more.

'Your lives weren't sad, just because you're dead now. You did funny things and laughed, just like we do — or did before we came to this place.' She laughed in surprise and astonishment at another photo. 'Look at the two of you!'

Phillip noticed that Julia's laughter was having a disturbing effect on the scorpion. It twitched, quivered. It raised its body on its back legs. Now it began to dance in an agitated way, as if it had been placed in a ring of fire. Julia laughed again. The ring of fire was the young girl's healthy, happy laughter. 'You were a couple of goofballs, Mum and Dad! Look at the two of you in fancy dress!'

She gave a peal of laughter, laughter that came from relief and forgiveness and warmth.

It was too much for the scorpion.

Its tail wound back like a catapult loading, then shot forward in a blur, aimed for a point behind the head — not Julia's, but its own. As the barb bit and poison crackled through its own body, it gave an enraged screech and vanished.

Julia got up, but she didn't close the book. She left it open. 'It's over now,' she said. 'It's an open book.'

15

Prisoner of the past

THEY REACHED A BROADENING of the river, a sort of delta region. Peering over the edge, Barry Coomber gave a shout: 'Hey, look everybody, there are people in the water — underneath the water.'

The others crammed to the edge of the boat. It was true. Drifting under the wavy ripples of the surface were the forms of men, unmoving men, drifting with the current. The ferryman explained. 'These are the drowned ones, the souls of men who have drowned in the Nile.'

'There are millions of them.'

'Many Egyptians could not swim and, since the Nile was their highway, and many travelled on it, many died in its waters.'

'How ghastly,' Julia said.

'There was special treatment for those who died in the Nile,' Willard told them. 'They were allowed to pass through the underworld to this stage even though they had missed the essential Egyptian burial.'

'I don't call this special treatment,' Barry Coomber said, pulling back from the edge.

Phillip looked morosely down at the shapes in the water. Without Dogstar and with hope dimming, he felt a bit like a drowned one himself. He wondered if he would be joining them before the journey was over.

It was time for Barry Coomber to face his test. He did not welcome Phillip's invitation to visit the hidden room of the deckhouse. 'I'm quite happy out here, thanks. I saw Julia's face when she came out of there. She looked pretty weird. She even smiled at me as she went past!'

'There's no choice. You have to go inside,' Phillip said. 'It's one of the tests. If you don't go inside, you fail. And that means we all fail. Don't you want to go home?'

'Okay, okay. And I suppose I have to go in there with you.'

'Go on your own if you like.'

'No, that's all right,' Coomber said, quickly. 'But I don't need you to hold my hand.'

'I wasn't planning to.'

Coomber shoved his hands in his pockets and went in at the forward door of the deckhouse. 'Smaller in here than I thought,' he said, looking around the antechamber.

'This isn't it. There's another door,' Phillip said, pointing. 'Go inside.'

'You want me to go first. Why? You've prepared a surprise for me. Is that it? The room's been booby trapped.'

'Don't be a booby,' Phillip said.

'You go in first.'

Phillip shrugged. 'Okay, but don't think you can

slip out of here. This is your challenge, not mine.'
Phillip went in first. Coomber followed a few steps
behind.

There was no column of light this time, nor sweet
smelling blue smoke; just a cone of light shining on a
small grille on the floor. It looked like a small ventilation grille set into the deck, but as Phillip went nearer,
he saw that it was an object sitting on top of the deck.
It was an oblong-shaped grille with a chrome shield in
the middle section which had transverse gills.

It was the front grille of a car. Mr Patrick's car. The
badge was missing.

'It's the front grille of an Alfa Romeo!' Phillip
whispered.

'No good to me; the badge is missing,' Barry Coomber said.

'I wonder why?'

'Don't ask me. I never took it. Don't need to. I've
got my own.' He performed a magic trick, drawing
the teacher's missing car badge out of Phillip's ear.
'Here's my one. That one's got nothing to do with me.'

'Oh yes, it has. It's here because you brought it here.
It was the same with Julia. This is the hidden room.
Each of us will find something different in the hidden
room, according to his need. In the hidden room we
will meet our secret fears, the past that we must face.'

'I don't have a past I've got to face.'

'Maybe you're right. Maybe you don't have to face
the past, like Julia did. Maybe you have to break away
from it.'

Coomber leaned against one of the columns. 'What
am I supposed to do?'

'I think you're supposed to put the badge back.'

'Why? It's my badge. I don't see why I should.'

'It's a test. If you fail, we're stuck here. You'll never see home again.'

'It's an illusion. I don't think it's real. How would an Alfa Romeo grille find its way into the deckhouse of an old Egyptian boat?'

'You brought it here in your mind.'

'Then if it's only in my mind, it isn't real. It's just a mirage — a hologram perhaps.' He went closer to the grille on the deck and squatted to examine it. He touched it, his hand passing into the cone of light. The falling light made bright strips of his outstretched fingers.

It was as if he had broken a beam that triggered a device. A cage with bars like the grille on the floor fell around him with the clang of a hundred prison gates slamming, leaving Phillip on one side and Barry Coomber trapped like an animal on the other.

Coomber threw himself at the bars and rattled them. 'I knew this was a booby trap. Let me out!'

'I didn't trap you. Can't you see? You've trapped yourself. You're trapped by your ways and by your past. You're going the same way as your brother Terry — and your father. You're going to end up in prison if you carry on stealing.'

'Trying to teach me a lesson, are you? Well, I don't want any teaching from you.' He gave the bars an angry kick. It hurt him. He hopped about on one foot, nursing his toe. Barry Coomber was in too much pain to see the serpent that slid down one of the columns from the inky blackness of the roof. It arranged itself in a curve around the grille on the floor.

'Look back.'

'I'm not interested in looking back. I told you there's nothing in my past I'm worried about.'

'Behind you, Coomber. There's something there.'

'What?'

'Look and see.'

A hissing sound filled the deckhouse and a shimmering sound of scales. 'I don't want to look.'

'Then take a look at the badge in your hand.'

'Why?'

'Look at it.'

Coomber reluctantly opened his hand to reveal the familiar symbol of the Alfa Romeo badge. It showed a red cross and beside it a serpent devouring something — was it a man with arms outspread? Or the handle of a sword?

'So?'

'What do you see?'

'The name "Alfa Romeo".'

'What else?'

'A cross and a serpent.'

'A cross and a devouring serpent. You have two choices. Follow one or the other, Coomber. But if you follow the serpent it's going to eat you.'

'Rubbish. There's nothing behind me.'

'Oh yes, there is. Your past. And your family's past. That's what's gaoling you.'

Barry Coomber turned very slowly to look behind him. The sight of the serpent with boot-button eyes gave him such a fright that he dropped the badge. It rolled across the deck and through the bars, ending up at Phillip's feet.

Phillip swept it up. He held it through the grille. 'Take it and put it back.'

'I'm not going near that thing.'

'It's only a monster of your mind. It can only harm you if you do what it wants. You must put the symbol back.'

Coomber threw his weight against the grille-like bars of the cage. He bounced off them. The bars didn't move. The serpent reared higher so that the top of its head was almost lost in darkness. 'It's going to strike!' Phillip said.

'Then help me, Phillip!'

'I can't. You can only help yourself. Ignore the mon-ster just as Julia did and it won't harm you, but you must overcome it. Do the right thing and return the badge.' He waved the badge between the bars in front of Coomber's face. 'Take the badge.'

'Do you think I can do that with a snake lying there?'

'You must. You mustn't be trapped by it. Just because your brother Terry and your father did wrong is no reason for you to copy them. You can break away from the past, but you must start now.'

'You're trying to get rid of me!'

'Do it — quickly!'

'All right.' Coomber took the badge. He turned and went towards the cone of light, but kept his head down so that he could not see the serpent's head that was reared above him. He looked bowed and guilty, like a child going forward to receive punishment.

The snake bent its head to look inquisitively down at the boy. Its scales in the dim light shone wetly like a dark street after rain. Its tongue threw silent lightn-ing into the air. Barry Coomber lost his nerve and stopped. He heard the hissing over his head. The serpent's scaled belly rose like tank's tracks ahead of him.

The serpent took aim to strike. 'Keep going!' Phillip said. 'Think of the cross, not the serpent.' Coomber stole a glance at the badge in his hand. It decided him. He edged nearer to the grille on the floor. He reached it and bent into the cone of light and held out the badge.

The Alfa Romeo emblem jumped out of his fingers as if sucked to the grille, clamping into position. At once the prison grille lifted off Barry Coomber and the snake slid away up a column, losing itself in darkness.

'Did I have to go through all that for a ten dollar badge?' Coomber said resentfully.

16

The loss of the past

PHILLIP WAS NEXT. He did not leave with Coomber, but remained in the hidden room to take his turn. The cone of light went out. Darkness wrapped itself around him. The darkness was cold and seeped into his clothes to reach his skin. The air in the room cleared and sweet-ened as if he were under open sky. He looked up and he saw a star in the sky.

Was it Sothis, the Dog Star? He heard a whine in the dark. It was directly ahead. He knew that whine. 'Dogstar, is that you?'

He heard another whine, this time from his left. He heard a clattering barking. He knew that bark. 'Dogstar, it *is* you. Come to me, boy. I want you back. That's all I want.'

The barking stopped.

A gentle light came on. It played on an earthen pottery bowl of water on the floor. The surface of the bowl drew Phillip's attention. It shone like a mirror. What kind of test was this? He went nearer; not afraid, but unsettled after hearing Dogstar. He looked into the bowl.

Things moved on the mirror surface. He saw Dogstar's face in the bowl, reflected as clearly as if the animal itself were leaning over the bowl. He dropped to his knees to peer into the bowl. The image of the dog vanished.

'Come back, boy,' he said.

It didn't, but another puzzling image appeared in its place. He saw a scene of struggle; a boy of his age at the edge of a deep pit, fighting against attackers, larger boys, who seemed to be trying to tear off his coat, a patchwork coat of bright colours. The older boys swiftly overpowered the smaller boy. They took his coat and threw him into the pit. They stood at the top of the pit and laughed. The boy in the pit pleaded with them.

Who were these people? They looked like Bedouin. The boy in the pit cried tears, making streaks in his dust-covered face. The boys at the top laughed, then without a wave they left.

Joseph with the coat of many colours. His jealous brothers threw him in a pit, leaving him to die, but seeing a passing caravan of traders they changed their minds and they sold him into slavery in Egypt. That was it. Midianite traders would come and the boy would be sold into slavery in Egypt.

The scene dissolved as though time had elapsed. The boy was growing weaker, clawing at the walls of the pit. The scene dissolved again and now the boy was still. That wasn't supposed to happen. Where were the Midianite traders who would take him to Egypt?

The scene vanished and clear water returned to the bowl. Phillip dipped a finger in the bowl. It was water, nothing more. He made ripples. The ripples settled. The surface returned to mirror calm. Then it changed colour. The water turned grey-green like the Nile.

Ripples again appeared on its surface as well as papyrus reeds at the edges — and into the reeds floated a rush basket. Inside the basket was a small pink form swaddled in a rough, peasant blanket. The basket drifted further into the reeds.

Phillip knew what would happen next. A daughter of Egypt would find the basket and draw it to the shore and bring up the baby as her own, little knowing that one day her adopted child would deliver the enslaved people of Israel from Egypt.

Reeds at the edge of the bowl parted. Was this the daughter of pharaoh reaching out for the floating basket? There was an explosion of green scales and saw-teeth as huge, green jaws took the basket and twisted, pulling it down into the swirling depths.

Crocodile.

'No,' Phillip protested. 'That's wrong. It can't happen. That baby is Moses. Where is the Egyptian princess?' The rush basket bobbed up again, now empty except for the peasant blanket. The basket sat low in the water. The wet blanket trailed in the water, gathering weight that would pull it back down. It drifted in the current and moved out of the scene. Moses, gone! It was impossible! It was shocking!

The bowl returned to silver emptiness.

Now the water turned to sand, to a scene of sand. A man, a woman and a baby were travelling hurriedly at night in the desert. The woman and the baby rode on a donkey and the man led the donkey on a rope.

The wind blew hard and the man leaned into it. The sand was soft and his feet slipped, but he did not rest.

He threw a glance over his shoulder, said something to the woman and quickened his pace. She looked back, holding her baby tightly and protectively. The baby, wrapped in a blanket in her arms, stirred as if whimpering.

Soldiers on horseback rode after the family. The man holding the donkey's rope broke into a run. The woman clutched the baby to herself. They stopped.

The desert had suddenly ended in nothingness.

They had come to the edge of a grey void. They looked ahead in desperation and baffled wonder. They tried to move into the void, but it blocked their way like a wall. They could go no further. They looked back, dread in their faces.

Soldiers on horses surrounded the couple and their baby. A man in a bronze helmet drew a sword from his scabbard and held out his hand for the baby. The woman cried in protest and clutched the baby tighter. The soldier snatched the baby from the woman, pulling her off the donkey. She fell onto the sand. Her husband ran to protect her. Another soldier struck him with the hilt of his sword and he fell beside the woman.

Phillip felt every nerve in his body rebel. He knew what he was seeing. It was the flight of the holy family to Egypt. They were fleeing to take shelter in Egypt, to save their baby from execution by King Herod. But they were supposed to escape. Why hadn't they reached Egypt?

There was to be no Egypt, that was why. Egypt *had* existed in all its glory — that was how Moses had come to be in the Nile, how the holy family had been travelling to Egypt — but it was disappearing in random pieces.

'No!' Phillip cried as if in pain. 'This can't happen! It mustn't. I won't let it!' He slammed the flat of his hand on the water's surface and sent it spraying over the deck.

It didn't make sense.

The boy with the coat had grown to become a high official of Egypt; the baby in the rushes had grown to become a prince of Egypt and the deliverer of his people; the baby in the arms of its mother had fled to Egypt and had grown up to reveal himself as the saviour of humankind.

Yet none of this happened in the scene.

Phillip had come to the underworld to save his dog, but now there was more than a dog to save.

He had to get back the scroll.

Suddenly ancient history wasn't just ancient history any more.

17

The final battle

'WE ARE ENTERING the twelfth hour of night,' the ferryman said as they went through a gateway. It wasn't a wall with pylons like the others, but the mouth of a cave. 'This is the final battle. We are entering the belly of the great serpent of the night and we must travel through the length of his body. If we survive we shall pass through his mouth and into the dawn.'

'Are you sure this isn't a cave?' Coomber said, twisting his head around. The light of their sunboat revealed oozy formations like flowstone on the walls.

'We are inside the great serpent,' the one whose face is turned backwards said. 'We are going through his body. The great serpent has swallowed the treasures of Egypt and it is here, in a great cavern of its belly, that you will find them.'

'And the scroll,' Phillip said. 'We've got to get back the scroll. We've got to stop Egypt from disappearing.'

Julia heard the shake of determination in Phillip's voice. 'How come you're so worried about the scroll? What about Dogstar?'

'They're one and the same problem.'

'You didn't think so before,' Willard Chase said.

'What happened to you in there?' Julia said.

'Never mind.'

'That's not fair. You know what happened to me. You went inside the hidden room with me.'

'And with me,' Coomber complained. 'A person can't get any privacy on this tub.'

'Remember the story you told the seekers of light about the light of the world? There is no story, and there is no light. . . unless we get back the scroll.'

'Tell me!'

'Not now. I'll tell you one day, but only if we can get back the scroll and stop a catastrophe from happening, the worst catastrophe in the history of the world.'

Phillip knew they were drawing close to the great cavern when soul birds swept low over the deck of the pyramid boat. He looked up at winged birds with human faces and painted eyes that glittered maliciously down.

'Leave this place, false shades! You will never take back the treasures of Egypt!'

Other soul birds appeared out of the darkness of the cave's ceiling, flying around their boat like sweeping clouds of bats, screeching and laughing in a squawking way. 'Soul birds. I remember them,' Julia said. 'They're the most ghastly things of all. Half bird, half person.'

'Watch your hair. They're spiteful and they'll pull it.'

Julia ducked just in time to avoid a soul bird making a grab for one of her swinging plaits. She screamed. More dived at her. Phillip found a spare oar on the deck and swung it like a sword.

The cloud of soul birds parted and broke around him, wheeling to return. Willard and Coomber, inspired by Phillip's example, looked around for weapons. Willard found a length of rope and Coomber a spar. They were ready for the next squadron of soul birds.

Willard cracked the rope end like a whip and a soul bird screamed in rage. Coomber clipped the tail feathers of another. One sunk its talons into Coomber's arm. Coomber gave a yell, dropping his spar. It only made him angrier. He picked it up again. 'Come and try that again,' he yelled after the laughing bird. 'I dare you.'

It declined the challenge. It joined the others, circling around the boat.

The travellers waited for another attack. It did not come. The soul birds flew off in formation.

The pyramid boat sailed further into the belly of the great serpent.

They followed a turn in the river, and there it was before them in the gloomy light: the ruined splendours of Egypt lay in a boundless cavern, scattered like playthings in a titan's toy cupboard.

Phillip's eyes shone at the sight of this the vast assembly of Egypt's past — shattered colossi of seated pharaohs in stone, obelisks of marble, pyramids, golden sarcophagi, caskets spilling over with jewellery, statues of men and of birds and animals, rolls of papyrus scrolls, chariots, golden bedsteads with leopard heads, parasols and ostrich feather fans, golden crooks and flails and frozen soul statues of dead kings with dark eyes staring from startling white orbits.

Above it all and further away lay the prize.

On a plinth, illuminated by a trickling light from above, sat an alabaster dog with a scroll between its paws.

Dogstar. Or at least a statue in the shape of Dogstar, Phillip thought. And between its paws, the magic scroll. Even at that distance, Phillip recognised it.

It was the scroll that dead Uncle William had unwisely taken to the grave with him, a scroll that had been his passport and sentence to the underworld, the scroll that had drawn Phillip through hell itself in a bid to rescue his uncle. Phillip had left the scroll behind and now it was a doorway to the real world, a doorway through which a malignant underworld had reached to plunder Egypt's heritage.

The ferryman guided their boat to the shore. 'Here you must go ashore and try to recover what you have come for. When you have recovered it, if you succeed, I shall be waiting for you at the mouth of the great serpent in the breath of the dawn.'

This part was going to be easy, Phillip thought. All they had to do was to go ashore and recover the scroll. 'Keep a watchful eye over your shoulder,' the man who looked backwards said.

'What for?' said Phillip. 'What can harm us now?'

'Egypt's past. Take care it does not rise from its long sleep to fight you.'

They went down the gangplank onto the shore. 'I don't know what he means,' Phillip said.

'I think I do,' Willard said. 'Let's stick together and keep our eyes on everything, especially those big guys in the stone chairs.'

'The statues of Rameses?'

'Got it. I don't want to scare you, but I think I saw their shoulders twitch.'

'Perfect,' Coomber said. 'Don't tell me this lot's going to come to life!'

Phillip threw a glance at the obscenely bulging stone legs at the base of the colossus. A smaller stone female figure, clinging to the calf of her powerful lord, turned empty socketed eyes to watch him pass. He hurried past.

'Hold it!' said Coomber. A gleaming golden snake that lay on a casket sat up and spread a jewelled hood warningly. It spat fire. Coomber ducked the flame. He grabbed a gold goblet and hurled it at the snake's head. It took cover in the cracked lid of a sarcophagus. 'Flame-throwing snakes! What next?'

'Don't look behind you.' There was a crumbling sound, then the thunderous crash of a landslide. Chunks of stone hit the ground and rolled around them. They twisted. Two seated colossi had climbed out of their stone chairs. By the looks of their massive clenched fists, they were not getting up to stretch their legs after a rest of a few thousand years.

'They're coming after us!'

The lid on a golden sarcophagus began to creak. Something inside lifted it and slid it aside. Bandaged hands reached out. A crumbling, tattered head rose to look at the group of tomb travellers.

They broke into a run.

A towering marble obelisk landed with a crash, meas-uring its length on the ground, shaking other objects around it. It blocked their way. It was too tall to climb. They ran around it. The footfalls of the colossi pursued them. *Thud, thud, thud.* The stone figures altered course to follow them. 'How can they see to follow us? They've got no eyes,' said Coomber complainingly.

They ran harder.

A leopard-headed bedstead with the legs and claws of a big cat ran into their path, the heads on the bedstead roaring a challenge. Coomber decided to try a little trampolining. He jumped into the middle of the bed, bouncing up and down like an expert, before sailing off the far side.

They heard the sound of tearing. A platoon of wooden Egyptian spearmen were ripping their feet free of the base on which they stood to attack the tomb travellers. A spearman broke free and let fly with his spear.

They ducked, taking cover behind an alabaster sphinx. The spear clattered harmlessly against its smooth surface. More spears rained against the alabaster.

Coomber and Willard grabbed fallen spears. The sphinx did not shelter them for long. It turned on the tomb travellers, its smooth stone muscles rippling, and it sat up on its base. It swiped at them with stone paws.

They jumped out of its range and ran on.

Soul birds dived from overhead. The travellers swung at them with their wooden spears. Phillip saw a sword handle protruding from a pile of tomb treasures. He armed himself with it. It was a bronze sword with a blade shaped like a feather.

They were drawing near to the plinth where the alabaster dog sat guarding the scroll between its paws.

An army was chasing them now. Phillip dared a

backwards glance over his shoulder at the stone colossi that were taking huge steps in pursuit. He saw a stone Rameses raise its foot and bring it down on a stone pyramid. Ouch, that would slow it down. It didn't. The pyramid turned to powder under the stone foot.

It spurred Phillip to run harder. Nearly there. Only one obstacle lay in their way now. A company of mummies had drawn up in a ragged line of horror to face them.

'We've got to fight our way through them,' said Willard, looking around anxiously.

'Yuk,' added Julia, but she stopped to sweep up a handy weapon, a gold ceremonial axe, from a pile of ceremonial weapons.

Willard and Coomber dropped their spears and did the same. They chose ceremonial swords.

'There must be hundreds of them,' said Coomber, looking aghast at the swaying line of mummies.

'More mummies than a mothers' club,' Willard joked.

'At least they're not armed.'

'Yeah, some don't even have arms,' Coomber said darkly, noting the gruesome fact.

'They don't need them,' Julia said. 'I think they plan to frighten us to death.'

The mummies began their advance. They chanted in dusty-sounding voices as they marched. It was a weary chant, all the more chilling for its empty-headed-ness.

What did the mummies plan to do? Was Julia right? Did these bandaged shells of former human beings hope to frighten the tomb travellers to death with a display of sheer mummery?

Our touch is much, our curse is worse;
Make no bones, we plan to fight. . .
We have no swords, our might is fright,
We're the tattered army of the night.
You can't hurt us, we don't bleed;
Of bandages we have no need. . .

'Yuk,' Julia said again, shuddering.

'Don't listen to their singing,' Phillip said. 'They're brainless. All mummies had their brains taken out in the mummification process.'

'He's right. They're only empty shells,' Willard said. 'But if we don't cut our way through them, they'll pile up and smother us with their dusty remains. Hack your way through them and don't worry; they can't feel a thing.'

Barry Coomber gave a war whoop and set on them first. He swung his ceremonial sword at an extended claw hand, then at a shoulder.

First a hand, now he grows bolder,
Takes my hand and then my shoulder. . .

Willard pushed another mummy aside with his boot and the boot went through the mummy's side.

Swing your blade, do your best —
See, you've only ripped my chest.

Julia closed her eyes and swung the golden axe at another advancing mummy. It chanted in a weary voice, even as the blade struck, throwing up powdery dust.

Hack in vain, slice me apart;
Strike all you like — I have no heart.

'Shut up!' Julia told it. 'Do you have to say these stupid things? You're supposed to be dead!'

Phillip cut off a powdery arm that grabbed at his shoulder.

Take my arm, it does no harm;
Break my head — I'm already dead!

Willard struck with his sword. They began to work a gap through the attackers. How did you know when you were winning against an army of mummies, against an enemy that was already in tatters? Phillip wondered.

He swung his feather-shaped sword at another.

'Together!' Willard said. The tomb travellers concentrated their attack and swung at the mummies. They broke through, scattering them. Mummies fell back on each other, toppling over like rows of dominoes.

Phillip ran to the plinth where the statue of Dogstar sat, the scroll lying between its paws.

The statue of the dog stirred.

Was it possible? It was a perfect copy of Dogstar, even to the neck where he saw the ring left by a collar and also the circular depression left by a municipal dog tag. Phillip snatched up the scroll. The dog cracked like a snake splitting, then shed flakes of alabaster skin. It launched itself off the plinth into Phillip's arms, knocking him to the ground, yelping in delight. Phillip rolled and rolled with the dog.

'Dogstar, you're back! Don't you ever go disappearing again, do you hear me?'

Dogstar licked the grime of battle off Phillip's face.

Then he noticed that the battle had gone quiet.

He turned. It was as if somebody had pulled out a battery or switched off the current in an amusement arcade. The mummies staggered drunkenly and fell over. A marching colossus slowed, frozen in midstep, and tumbled over, shaking the ground like an earthquake. The other one fell on top of it and broke. Slithering golden snakes and crawling creatures rolled over onto their backs, showing their bellies. Obelisks crashed like chopped-down trees.

The tomb travellers gathered in a ring around Phillip, breathless from the battle, but lit up with smiles of relief — and even Barry Coomber looked pleased with his efforts.

They had the scroll. And Phillip had Dogstar.

Nothing could stop them now, Phillip thought. The tomb travellers were together again — all of them. The underworld had done its worst and failed!

'I wouldn't let them take you, 'Star boy. And now I'm going to do something I promised I'd do.' Phillip dug into a pocket and took out the small leather loop with a municipal registration tag attached. He put it around the dog's tapered neck and fastened it and the dog licked his arm gratefully. 'There, you're mine again. It's only a small band, but it tied us together and not even eternity could break it.'

Julia was crying and laughing all at once.

18

The dawn

THEY REJOINED THE BOAT. Tiredness had crept over their bodies and minds. Phillip curled up with Dogstar on the deck, a contented smile on his face, and the others stretched out nearby. Dogstar licked Phillip's nose before they both fell asleep.

The boat rocked gently. What boat? Phillip thought. It wasn't a boat. It was the bed. Something had climbed onto Phillip's bed. He opened his eyes. Dogstar was on the covers, licking his face. The morning sun threw yellow squares on his bedroom wall.

Dogstar barked.

Phillip sat up. Dogstar's paws were covered with mud. 'Where's the scroll? And where's the bird, boy? What have you done with them? You haven't gone burying things again, have you? You mustn't bury the past. It matters, after all.'

Dogstar's tongue lolled from its mouth and it seemed to have a grin on its face. The sly hound!

Phillip lay back. He was too tired to think about the problem just yet.

He thought instead about Julia and Barry Coomber

and Willard Chase and the ferryman. He wondered, as dreamers do when they have dreamt of others, whether they would somehow know it and remember what had happened.

He patted Dogstar's head. 'Well at least we made it to the morning, 'Star boy.'

Did she remember, Phillip thought, looking at the clean profile of Julia who sat at the desk beside him. Did Coomber?

'Patchy's coming.'

A car drove up slowly and pulled up carefully in the teacher's parking lot outside the classroom. Mr Patrick came in. He looked a lot more friendly than last time. His face was still the colour and texture of porridge, but this time it was warm porridge and it was even sprinkled with a little sweetness.

'Good morning, history lovers,' he said pleasantly.

'Good morning, Mr Patrick,' they said.

'A bit of history happened overnight,' Mr Patrick said to the class, peeling off his favourite sports jacket with the patches at the elbows and hanging it up carefully on a hook. 'A miracle if you like. Do you remember how the grille badge went missing off my car? Well somehow, mysteriously, a badge has reappeared on my grille. Stuck back in place, if you don't mind.

'But here's the strangest part. It's not the same badge. It's a brand new one. My old badge had a scratch on it, you see, so I know. The genius who stole it decided to replace it with a brand new one. Nice of him. In fact, a commendable use of pocket money, if I may say so.'

The tips of Barry Coomber's ears glowed redly. He must have felt the stares from Phillip and Julia, but he kept looking straight ahead.

After the lesson, Julia leaned sideways in her desk. 'What are you doing at break-time, Phillip?' she said.

'Not much. I thought I might stroll over to the library and look at some books on ancient Egypt. Why?'

'I wanted to show you something, that's all. But it doesn't matter,' she said, although clearly disappointed.

'What?'

She raised the lid of her desk and took out a blue photographic album with a brass ring binder. 'You wanted to see a picture of my mum and dad. I decided to show you.'

'Good for you, Jool! What changed your mind?'

She shook her head, swinging the plaits on the sides of her head. 'I don't exactly know, Phillip. But I did have the strangest dream about these pictures. I had a dream that a creepy insect was sitting on the cover of my album. Dancing on it, actually. It was a scorpion, I think. I can't be sure.

'Anyway, I woke up this morning and I knew that I had to open the album. I don't know what made me do it — or what stopped me from doing it before. It was perfectly easy and I feel better for doing it.'

They joined the queue of students going out of the classroom. They met Coomber at the door. He pushed past the two of them even more rudely than usual, anxious to avoid them.

'Nice of you to buy Patchy a new badge,' Phillip said after him.

'Why would I do a dumb thing like that?' Coomber

flung back irritably.

'Yes, I'm curious about it, too,' Julia said to Coomber in a puzzled voice. 'Why didn't you just give Mr Patrick the original one?'

'I don't have it.' He walked away down the corridor.

'But he did have it,' Julia said to Phillip. 'We saw him take it out of his ear in class.'

'Perhaps he left it somewhere,' Phillip said.

They went out of the classroom and into the bright sunshine. Julia was carrying the blue album under her arm. Phillip would look at the photographs with her. He could always go to the library and read about ancient Egypt another time. Egypt could wait. After all, it wasn't going to disappear.

Other books by Roy Pond
published as Albatross
teenage paperbacks:

PLAYING DIRECTOR

Dave loved reading choose-
your-own story books. He
didn't like others deciding
which way his favourite
stories should go.

Then one day he met a movie director while on the
Ghan train to Australia's centre. 'You pretend I don't
exist if you like, but I'm here and I plan to share the
journey with you.'

Dave looked up from the page of his choose-your-
own story book into the eyes of a bearded stranger.

'You like being in control?' the movie director said.

What an exciting, yet scary possibility! Dave could
play director of his own life — choose his own path,
his own endings. No longer the humdrum, the boring,
the same old routine, but adventure in the mysterious
red heart of Australia, riding a legendary desert train.

But what if he chose the wrong track?

REMOTE CONTROL

'What if I said you were looking at Flite Madison in the flesh?' the flier said.

'I'd laugh. He's a book hero.'

'Maybe. But the books could have been written about me. I'm just like him. I fly anthing, anywhere, and never ask too many questions — just like Flite Madison.'

Was the flier Nick's long-sought hero? Who better for a model plane enthusiast? And didn't Nick's English teacher say he needed more experience of life to write? Should he stay on the ground and 'play it safe', or join the flier and take a few risks.

TOMB TRAVELLERS

The first of the tomb travellers' exploits in ancient Egypt, this adventure starts with Phillip's fascination with the past.

When his Uncle William, an Egyptologist, dies, his copy of the *Book of the Dead*, a passport to the Egyptian afterlife, is buried with him. Is that where he's gone? Can Phillip find him there?

In Phillip's mind, an ancient world unfolds. Dangerous curiosity leads Phillip and his friends to the gateways and guardians of Egypt's forbidden underworld. But to escape they must pass many tests!